Yellow Gulch Law

John Russell Fearn

1. The Square 8 Ranch

"Well, Shorty, there it is, I reckon."

Jess Burton brought his powerful sorrel to a halt, hipped round in the saddle, and surveyed the scenery. It was still early in the morning, only a few hours past dawn, and Arizona was awakening to a new Spring day. The two men high up on the rimrock saw the glorious Mariposa tulips lifting their orange cups and the sweetpea blossoms creeping over a violet carpet of hyptis and verbena. The very perfume in the air was life itself.

But Nature's beauty had nothing in common with the valley into which the two men looked. A ranch sprawled there, with extensive corrals penning some five thousand head. Down there at the Square-8 lived Wilton de Brock, self-styled cattle emperor and overlord of the entire small state of Yellow Gulch. The brutal dominance of Wilton de Brock was something of which most men and women knew, from the lowliest cattle-tenders on the far-flung ranches of these mighty spaces, to the wealthy cattle-owners, themselves. The tales told of him were varied, but they added up to the same thing: he made his own laws and had the power to enforce them. Yellow Gulch was de Brock's property and he ran it in his own way.

There were dozens of such semi-feudal territories scattered throughout the vast American continent, for the great United States of America was as yet only a dream. Men fought and lived and died by their guns — and Wilton de Brock could outshoot the fastest of them.

"Well, what d'you think of it?" Jess Burton asked at length, in his slow but powerful voice.

He was a tall, rangy man in the mid-thirties, his exposed skin a burned-in brown, his eyes deep blue, his cheekbones high. Though he did not smile readily, his face was likeable.

"Good enough, I guess," his short, tubby companion answered, cuffing up his Stetson on to his forehead. "Leastways it should be better'n kickin' around in th' desert an' goin' no place in partic'lar. Ain't much fun in bein' lone rangers … "

Shorty Pearson reflected for a moment, his pale, grey eyes travelling over the scene, then he added: "Jus' th' same, Jess, there is somethin' worth havin' in the open sky an' th' wide spaces. Mebby it's better'n bein' cooped up an' doin' as yore told. I s'pose it all depends if that guy de Brock's willin' t' take us on, doesn't it?"

"Yeah — but there's no reason why he shouldn't. What we don't know 'bout cow-pokin' ain't worth mentionin'."

"Jus' th' same, frum what I've heard uv de Brock, cow-punchin' mebby ain't th' only thing he wants. He's a tough character, an' afore we're finished, 'specially the way you talk, anythin' might happen."

Jess grinned. "Anyways, let's be seein' what we can do about it."

He spurred his sorrel and set the animal sweeping down the grassy valley side. Only a few yards behind him came Shorty, presently catching up. As they rode together both men became aware of signs of activity about the Square-8 spread. Men were going back and forth in the huge corrals and across the main yard. A

4

wagon and team was being prepared for a journey, probably into the two mile distant town of Yellow Gulch itself.

When he reached the gateway of the yard he drew his mount to a halt and hailed one of the punchers nearby, who turned and came ambling forward slowly.

"How does a feller get to see de Brock?" Jess enquired.

"Mostly, he doesn't," the cowpoke answered, squinting up into the sunlight. "Depends on what yore hankerin' after."

"Jobs for me an' my pardner here. We heard back along th' desert trail that de Brock was takin' on new hands for his outfit, so we rode over."

"Best thing yuh can do is go up to the ranch-house an' ask if he'll see yuh," the puncher suggested.

Jess nodded, jerked his head to Shorty, and together they rode across the wide yard. Leaving their horses tethered to the tie-rack, they mounted the three steps to the porch and Jess thumped on the screen-door. A square-shouldered hard-faced woman of middle age presently arrived to deal with them. There was a certain suspicion in her expression as she surveyed the two men.

"Well?" she asked briefly.

"Mornin', ma'm." Jess touched his hat brim. "We were wonderin' if Mr de Brock's still takin' on hands for this spread of his. We're both — "

"Saddle tramps, by the looks of you!"

Jess eyed the woman levelly. "I reckon you can't ride the trail for long hours around here, ma'm, without getting' a mite dirty. Still, if there isn't anythin' we can do around here we can ride further, an' thanks for — "

"I'm not turning you away," the woman interrupted. "Just sizin' you up, that's all. You'd best ask my husband for yourselves." She drew the door open wider. "Walk straight across the hall and into th' living room there."

"Thank you kindly, ma'm." Tugging off his hat Jess led the way and entered the room the woman had indicated.

It was comfortably furnished in the log-wall, skin-rug style. At a broad desk near the window an ox-shouldered man with close-cropped grey hair sat writing. He only looked up when Jess and Shorty were facing him across a pile of papers and correspondence.

"Well?" he asked curtly — and sat back in his chair.

Wilton de Brock was probably fifty years of age, as solidly power-packed as one of his own stallions. His head was perfectly round, a fact rendered even more noticeable by his scrub haircut. Square features, verging on the cruel, were deeply sun-tanned. His eyes were glacial blue, so light that with the morning sunshine catching them diagonally they appeared transparent.

Here, Jess decided, was a man who loved power for power's sake, and who was not particularly concerned as to how he gained or maintained it.

"Do you have to stand there all day!" he demanded at length, and it seemed queer in such a man to find his voice smooth and well educated.

"Er — sorry," Jess apologized, holding his hat by the brim in front of him. "I'm Jess Burton and this is my sidekick "Shorty" Pearson. We're looking for jobs. We heard you were extending your outfit."

"Where did you hear it?" de Brock asked curtly. "I'm not in the habit of advertising my activities."

"Ways back on the trail. A guy by the name of Cornish. Said he'd been in your outfit but that you'd fired him. He told us you were taking on hands, so havin' nothing particular in mind we figured we might as well ride in and see if we could do anything. Just being footloose can get tirin'."

Wilton de Brock gave a hard grin. "For your edification, Burton, Cornish was not fired. He ran away! I found it necessary to exercise certain disciplinary measures and — well, he turned yellow and bolted. However, that is neither here nor there. Where are you from? What can you do? Your appearance isn't exactly neat."

"I guess neither of us are from anywheres particular," Jess responded. "We've just bin roaming around for the last three years. Last regular job we had was at the Straight-J back in Kansas. We got sick of livin' to rule, though, and decided to hit leather — but like I said it's a hard life roamin' around with nothin' to fix your mind on but desert — "

"In other words, you're hombres? Saddle tramps?"

A glint came and went in Jess' bright blue eyes but his tone remained respectful. "I guess so," he admitted, "but we can handle steers an' we know all the runs of a layout like yours. Whether the spread's big or little makes no odds to us."

The pale, cruel eyes flashed to Shorty and pinned him. Shorty swallowed to himself and waited.

"What about you, Pearson? Just plain dumb or incapable of speaking for yourself?"

"Course I ain't," Shorty retorted. "Just don't seem no sense in two of us talkin' when Jess can do it for th' both of us. He always did do the talkin' in our team."

"Very logical," the cattle baron agreed, with a dry grin. "I may as well tell you two men that I don't like saddle tramps in my outfit because I don't trust them, but it so happens that I have regulations and laws which prevent any doublecrossing, thieving, or gunplay. In plain words, all my men are equal, that is, amongst those who do the hard work. There are bosses to whom they're answerable; and they in turn are answerable to me. You understand?"

"You mean," Jess said slowly, "that if we are crazy enough to think of gettin' smart ideas you'd bushwhack us afore we could turn round?"

"That's just what I mean, and it's as well for you to grasp the fact from the start. My foreman, Clint Andrews, is well paid to see that my orders are carried out. That being so I'm willing to give you two desert rats a trial. You'll get five dollars a week each and your keep."

Jess and Shorty exchanged glances; de Brock's cold eyes switched from one to the other.

"If you don't like it you can get off this territory," he said briefly. "I didn't ask you to join my outfit, remember. In fact I'm doing you a favour taking you on at all."

"It's a mighty low wage," Jess said bluntly.

"What do you expect for cow-poking? A fortune?"

"No, just enough dollars to make a living, and that isn't my idea of it," Jess' voice slowed and he gave a

8

shrug. "Just the same it's better 'n the desert and wandering, I suppose ... Okay, we'll take it."

"You'll find Clint Andrews somewhere about outside," de Brock said. "If you've any complaints to make see him about them. I haven't the time to deal with them. Just one thing I would add — don't complain unless you have to. Clint doesn't like grousers."

Without further words Jess and Shorty left the ranch-house, glancing at each other significantly as they went. They had gained the yard again and were standing beside their horses before Shorty made a comment.

"I dunno that you'd call me the anti-social type," he said, spitting casually into the dust, "but there's somethin' about that jigger de Brock which I don't like. Seems to me that all th' things that've been sed about him have bin true. The guy's a low-down, an' all th' worse for bein' rich an' powerful into th' bargain."

"Yeah ... " Jess gave a sigh. "However, since we've very little money, Shorty, and even less prospects, I guess we'd better go th' way of the wind, leastways for the time being. Better be finding that foreman, hadn't we?"

They came upon him eventually in the midst of the job of branding yearlings. Their mournful bleatings mixed with the stench of scorching hair and hide. Jess stood watching for a while, his eyes narrowing a little as he saw the unnecessary cruelty with which the young animals were being treated.

Suddenly he started forward with little strides, his fists clenched at his sides.

There ain't no call for tying that steer's back and front legs," he snapped abruptly. It's simpler to — "

9

"You tellin' me what t' do, stranger?" The foreman stood up, throwing the smoking branding-iron back in the brazier again. He grinned crookedly. If so, I shouldn't. It ain't healthy to do that around here."

Jess hesitated, not because he was afraid of the broad-shouldered, thick-featured giant in front of him but because he wanted a job. It was no use ruining his and Shorty's chances before they had even got started.

"You Clint Andrews?" Jess asked.

"Yeah. What about it?"

"Mr de Brock told us to report to you."

The foreman grinned all the wider and put his hands on his hips.

"He did, huh? Well, ain't that nice! Couldn't suit me better than t' have a wise guy workin' under me."

"I don't work for anybody 'less he plays the game straight," Jess snapped.

The foreman spat and then considered. "I guess I've broken in better men'n you, feller, as you may find out before long. Til lay off yuh this time 'cos yore new, but don't go shootin' your face off too much. I mightn't like it."

Jess hesitated and then slowly he relaxed. Keeping his temper had always been his hardest task.

"Guess I'm a bit edgy," he muttered. "Bin doin' a lot of hard riding lately."

"Okay. Then you can make yourself really tired by clearin' out them sheds over there. I reckon we ain't so partic'lar about stinks around here as a rule, but them sheds is more than even we can stick. Get busy, an' make 'em clean!"

Jess turned, jerked his head, and Shorty followed him in the direction of the outhouses. The odour from within retched their stomachs, but they went to work just the same, their kerchiefs tied about their faces … And this job was only the first. By the end of a gruelling, sizzling day they had done practically every dirty job which the foreman could rake up. Their tempers were not improved in consequence.

It was after supper in the bunkhouse, with the rest of the outfit gathered around him, that Jess let himself go. Since the foreman was not present it did not seem to him that it mattered if he let off steam.

"How do you fellers stick it!" he demanded, looking about him. "What kind of a spread does this guy de Brock think he's running, anyway? I guess even convicts get better treatment than this. Even the food stinks."

He whipped up the remains of his meal, which he had not been able to tolerate, and flung it on the floor. The oozing mass stuck to the unwashed boards. For a while there was dead silence and the men looked grimly at each other.

"Ain't healthy to argue about it," a cowpoke remarked. "Or don't yuh know, stranger, jus' how much power de Brock's got in these parts?"

"Course I know!" Jess retorted. "His name stinks from one end of the country to the other, and I can plainly see why now. However much power he's got it doesn't entitle him to treat us like pigs!"

"Mebbe not," the cowpoke agreed, "but who's t' stop him gettin' away with it? He's the law throughout this entire territory an' there ain't no other."

"There's a certain amount of State law in being," Jess snapped. "A man can't do just as he likes without gettin' one of the State Governors down on him mighty quick. I guess de Brock's illegal methods must be known to the authorities, but they're hogtied without proof. Just the same, it seems a visit from one of them, say from North Point City, is a long way overdue."

One of the men chuckled, a big, lumbering giant of a man with a plug-ugly face and unruly black hair.

"What's so funny?" Jess demanded, wheeling on him.

"Just one thing, stranger. One or two folks got the same notion as you an' tried to get a Governor down here from North Point. They figgered they could get through as living proof of de Brock's ill treatment, but though that city's only fifty mile away the stunt didn't work. Those who tried it was ambushed afore they could finish. If yuh want t' keep your health, feller, yuh'd best start in realizin' that Wilton de Brock is th' be-all and end-all hereabouts."

Jess was silent for a while, thinking, and looking across to where the big fellow was lounging on a hard chair, its back propped against the wooden wall.

"Ever hear of Joe Cornish?" Jess asked presently.

"Sure," the big fellow assented. "He usta work in this outfit. One uv de Brock's paid spies an' gunmen. One uv the nastiest characters I ever happened on."

Jess gave a start and glanced at Shorty, then back to the big fellow.

"How'd you mean?" Jess questioned. "I used to know Cornish some years ago an' he was a straight-shooter enough then. It was because of that I took his word for it when he told me an' Shorty that de Brock was wantin' men for his spread. If it hadn't have bin for him we wouldn't have come."

The ironic laughter which broke out made Jess frown.

"What gives?" he asked coldly, looking about him. You boys mean that Shorty an' me were tricked into comin' here?"

"Yeah, that's it." The big fellow got to his feet and, his thumbs latched in his pant's belt, came ambling over to where Jess had sat on the long table, "de Brock is such a tyrant that he can't git any labour the straight way, so th' only other method is to hi-jack whoever he can get. Some of th' men who are as ornery as he is rake in workers where they can. An' Cornish is just such a man. In a word, feller, yuh wus sold out to de Brock."

Jess was silent, his lips tight, a glitter in his blue eyes.

The big fellow looked at him for a moment, then added: "Yore here now, an' th' only way yuh'll ever get out of the territory, where you might spread information as to what goes on here, is feet first, with a slug in your heart. Since others have tried it an' gotten themselves bushwhacked there's no reason for supposin' yuh could do any better."

"Mmmm …" Jess' eyes narrowed. "Which explains what de Brock meant when he talked of discipline an' regulations … An' you guys here stand for it, do you?" he demanded, looking around him again and frowning.

"Becos we ain't plain crazy, yes," another puncher said. "If we try anythin' we either git flogged or solitary without water fur four days. That ain't worth riskin'. Best do as yore told, collect what bit o' money is comin' to yuh, an' shut your eyes an' ears to everythin' else.

Mebby not exactly as we'd like it, but we stay sorta healthy."

"On the kind of muck this heel gives us to eat?" Jess snapped. "I'd sooner starve to death!"

"Guess that's what yuh will do, feller, if yuh don't eat what's set before yuh."

The big fellow gave a grim smile. "Which gives yuh some idea, stranger, uv the kind uv yellow-bellies I haveta mix with! I'd break out tomorrow an' wipe out de Brock, Clint Andrews, an' all th' rest uv the stinkin' bunch, if I could." He looked over the assembly with narrowed eyes, his ugly face set in arrogant contempt. "But I guess I can't do it single-handed."

"Mebby you won't have to," Jess said quietly. "I've seen enough in one day to satisfy me that I don't like this place: it's too much like a penal settlement. An' when I choose to hit th' trail it'll take a stronger man than de Brock to pin me down."

"That's my language too, feller." The big cowpuncher rubbed his massive hands together; then he held one forward impulsively in welcome. "Nixon's th' monicker," he said, his ugly face lighting in a grin, "but most folks call me 'Ox'."

"Okay, Ox it is." Jess shook hands. "I'm Jess Burton. This is Shorty Pearson. Whilst we're about it, Ox, tell me more. What exactly goes on in this territory? What's de Brock driving at? Is he just a plain tyrant or has he some object in his roughshod methods?"

"Bit of each, I reckon." Ox squatted on the table beside Jess and became thoughtful for a moment or two. Then he went on: "All of us boys here have bin more or less roped in to work fur him through hi-jackin', an' so far

14

we ain't done nothing about it. In this region th' sheriff an' mayor is both in de Brock's pay, so they shut their eyes to anythin' that goes on. Anybody sayin' anythin' against the skunk is usually strung up. His aim is to run not only this partic'lar territory of Yellow Gulch, but all Arizona afore he's through."

"When, an' if, a Union comes inter bein' he reckons to be one uv th' most powerful men in it. Becost of that hope he's extendin' his power everywheres. All his cattle deals is illegal an' nobody can stop it. A lot uv his steers have bin rustled from the neighourin' ranches in th' territory. What he really aims at is t' drive every settler outa th' region, either by persuasion or open violence, an' unless I'm plain loco he'll do it afore he's finished."

"Nice feller," Jess commented, sighing. "And what good will that do him? The settlers have bought the land from him, haven't they? They must have some say in the matter, or are they too plumb scared of this skunk to say so?"

"Ain't quite that way," Ox replied. "The settlers bought th' land from Amos Crand, who wus the sort uv boss around here before de Brock blew in with his owl-hooters an' rubbed out Crand an' everybody connected with him. de Brock's idea is to drive th' settlers out, reclaim the land fur himself, an' then sell it at the highest price if a Union comes, as looks mighty likely one day."

Ox spat on the floor and lighted the cigarette he had been rolling whilst talking.

"Now yuh see what we're up against," he said, musing amidst the fumes. "An' believe me, feller, I'd risk most anythin' t' rub out th' dirty skunk, an' as I see it yore uv the same notion."

"As nice a setup as I've struck in some time," Jess said, pondering. "Seems like the stories that have been spread around aren't so exaggerated."

"You sed it," Ox agreed.

"What it amounts to is that the settlers around here are in fear of their lives and against de Brock's hired gunmen they don't stand a chance? Nobody to protect their interests. That the trouble?"

"That's it. Those who've tried t' break away an' get help to this territory have bin wiped out, like I told yuh. Position ain't so much better for us. Yuh notice none uv us is allowed to keep guns, an' there's guards around outside who keep a watch on anybody tryin' t' make a break from this outfit. Once in this area, feller, yore in it fur keeps less you've the brains to get out." Ox gave a wide grin. "I don't reckon t' have any brains meself. My fists have always gotten me through, but you look as if yuh might have a head on yuh."

"Thanks," Jess conceded dryly. "Just the same you've been here longer than I have. You must have made some kind of plan in that time."

"Nope. It weren't any use makin' any with these yellow-bellies refusin' t' back me up if I tried somethin', so I just got around to leavin' things alone 'til somethin' happened I could make use uv."

Ox looked about him sourly and one or two of the men shifted uneasily. Jess looked about him, too: then he said quietly:

"Look, you fellers. If Ox an' me found a way to get clear of here would you support us?"

"Not if they've any blasted sense!" a voice commented.

Every man turned, Jess and Ox included. Clint Andrews was in the doorway of the bunkhouse, a heavy .45 in his hand. With cold menace on his thick features he came forward slowly, the floorboards creaking under his weight. When he arrived at the food Jess had flung down he regarded it ominously, then moved his attention to the set-faced men gathered around him.

"Who around here don't like the menu we serve?" he demanded.

Nobody answered. The men looked at each other and some of them folded their arms. Andrews' left hand rested casually on a leather butt tucked in his belt, then suddenly with a blast of rage he ripped the butt out, a lashing whiptail on the end of it. Its cutting thong belaboured the backs and faces of the nearest men, Ox and Jess included.

"Stand here like a lot of dumb swine, eh?" Clint Andrews screamed. "By hell, we'll see about that! Answer me, damn you!"

Still nobody said anything, but in the eyes of Jess there was bleak murder. Unnoticed, he reached down into the back of his half-boot and gripped the handle of a thin, wickedly sharp dagger. He waited in smouldering calm until the foreman came to the peak of his blind fury, raising his lash again. Then Jess acted.

His knife slashed up and down again, a briefly glinting line in the oil lights. It was so swift an action hardly anybody saw what happened. But Clint Andrews crashed to the floor, blood soddening his shirt across the left breast. His whip fell a few feet away, his gun slid into a corner. Not two yards from his head was the plate of down-flung food.

There was hard breathing, the men looking tensely at one another. Slowly Jess slipped the knife back into his half-boot and drew the back of his hand over his sweating forehead.

"One place they didn't think t' look for a weapon," he said.

"You didn't oughta have done that, feller," a puncher whispered, his eyes popping.

"It'll mean th' rope," another said, staring. "Looks like yuh've killed Clint."

"Yeah," Ox breathed, staring down at the foreman as though hypnotized.

"I reckon one could call it justifiable homicide," Jess said, his voice steel-hard. "A man like Clint Andrews wasn't fit to be in charge of an outfit. In fact he wasn't fit t' live at all. I'm not regrettin' my action one little bit. Pity is somebody didn't do it sooner."

"Git him outa sight, an' fur th' love of God hurry it up!" gasped a puncher near the doorway. "Somebody's a-comin'. Mebby de Brock himself."

It was, and there was no time to shift the dead foreman's sprawled body, or to make a dash for his fallen gun. The cattle baron came into the bunkhouse and looked about him. Such was the iron-hand control of the man over his emotions he did not even blink when he saw the foreman. Instead he halted and stood with his head on one side, considering.

"So," he remarked at length. "In spite of all the warnings you have had, and knowledge of the dire consequences following any infraction of orders, one of you found it necessary to play games!"

There was no response. The men stood looking at him whilst his transparent eyes flashed from one to the other. Then he came forward again, his hand resting on the butt of his gun. He moved with a swagger, but every nerve was obviously taut for action.

"Needless to remark," he resumed, his voice so low and deadly it was hardly audible, "I have no liking for talking to myself. I asked you men a question, and I'll give you five seconds in which to answer. If you prefer not to take advantage of my leniency I will see that each one of you is flogged without mercy until one or other of you breaks and tells me the facts. Believe me, I will get the truth out of you no matter how much you suffer or how long I have to wait."

He removed a costly watch from his fancy vest and contemplated it, withal keeping a wary eye on the men about him.

"One … two … " He began to count relentlessly.

Still nobody spoke. Jess sat on the table edge with his mouth taut. Ox rolled himself a second cigarette and lighted it deliberately. Shorty kept his arms folded, a look of sour disgust on his whiskery visage.

"Very well," de Brock said finally, as the fifth second passed. "You have only yourselves to thank."

He raised his voice in a shout and through the doorway two gunmen came hurrying in. They halted in their sudden forward rush and stared, first at the body on the floor and then at their boss.

"Take this muscle-bound ape and deal with him," de Brock directed them curtly, dashing Ox's cigarette from his mouth to the floor and grinding it under his heel. "He's been trying for long enough to make trouble around here, and this time it seems he's gotten away with it. At the end of thirty lashes he may be inclined to speak. I've been awaiting a chance like this for a long time. Now I may consider it legitimate to hammer some obedience into his thick hide."

"Me?" Ox gasped, staring. "But I never — "

"Shut up and start moving!" de Brock ordered, his gun leaping into his hand. "Outside! Same applies to the rest of you. You can watch what happens and gain some idea of what is coming to each one of you. Maybe you'll learn to have better sense in the future."

Bewildered and swearing, Ox found himself menaced by three guns, two of them belonging to the leather-necked guards. He was bundled out into the big yard, his shirt stripped from him, then he was forced to double over a large horizontal barrel. Ropes were tied round his wrists and were then drawn taut under the barrel to his ankles on the opposite side. Thus-wise his massive naked back was completely exposed.

The assembled men stood watching, their faces grim.

"Before we start," de Brock said levelly, eyeing the gathering in the glow of kerosene light from the ranch-house porch, "you should know that this is justice. Scum like you will never speak through ordinary persuasion. Once I know the guilty man the flogging will cease and the culprit will be dealt with — by hanging."

"By what right do you make laws?" Burton snapped, and the cattle-baron gave him a snakelike stare.

"By the right that in this state I, Wilton de Brock, am the only master. I make the laws and administer them to

20

the full. No more, no less. All right?" he finished, nodding to his gunmen, "get on with the job, and don't spare yourselves, either. He's tough enough to stand it."

The two guards holstered their guns and from their belts took short-tailed whips. Before they could start, however, Jess stepped forward.

"Hold it!" he said briefly. "There's no need for any of this. I'm the man you want, de Brock."

The cattle baron considered him. "You are, are you? A man of unusual violence for a newcomer to our little community, eh? Though from the amount you have had to say I suppose I should not be surprised."

"I wiped out Clint Andrews because he wasn't fit to live. It was as simple as that."

"I see. It so happens, however, that I have a great dislike of having my hired men eliminated so drastically. It upsets all my arrangements."

Jess said nothing. He was preparing for a spring, but the slow tautening of his muscles was not visible in the dim light. Then, as de Brock remained silent Jess resumed talking:

"It seems, de Brock, that so far no man around here — save mebby Ox — has had the guts to stand up to you and your damned sadism. But it's going to change."

"Is it really?"

"Yeah, and right now!"

Jess dived suddenly and with overwhelming force. His right fist came up as he moved, and behind it was all the power of his muscles, de Brock took the blow under the jaw and staggered helplessly backwards into the dust, his gun flying out of his hand. He twisted and made a frantic effort to seize it, but before he could do so he realized that the point of a glinting knife was at his jugular.

2. Breaking Loose

"Take it easy," Jess warned, pinning the cattle baron down. "Since I didn't think twice about blotting out Andrews, there's no reason why I shouldn't do the same with you, is there? In fact you're a bigger plum than he could ever ha' been."

"All right, get on with it!" de Brock muttered, and just for a moment Jess had to admire the man's cynical courage, with death only a hair's breadth from him. "Or perhaps I have the wrong idea and you have some reason for allowing me to live?"

"Yeah, sure I have. I'm not lettin' you have a swift grand exit after the way you've been behavin' in the territory."

"Stop fooling around, man, and come to the point!" de Brock panted.

"I will, in my own time. Y' see, de Brock, you've gotta learn the hard way and see your whole tinhorn empire come crashin' down around your ears, before you finally get yourself blotted out. I sort of figger I'm the man who can deal with that — along with a few others. Yore livin', de Brock, just so's you can die more slowly from here on. That, to me, seems nice an' poetic."

"You don't know the kind of man yore fightin'," de Brock said, his colourless eyes aimed upwards. "But, by God, you will before you're finished! And I mean finished!"

I'm willin' to put that to the test. I may change my mind and slit your throat right now unless you give some orders. First of all get Ox released." de Brock gave the order, his voice hoarse. Ox, the ropes unfastened, stood up from the barrel and dragged on his shirt. Then he looked at the two guards who had released him. He sized them up slowly, his big mouth set in brutal hardness.

"Yuh cheap, low-down ornery skunks," he whispered. "Tickin' on a jigger who's got no guns, huh? Seems like the pair uv yuh is about due fur repayment."

With battering ram impact his left and right fists shot out, knocking each guard backwards one after the other. As they collapsed in the dust Ox whipped up their guns into his own powerful hands.

"Okay!" he shouted. "Since Clint Andrews got what wus comin' to him there ain't no reason why you gorillas shouldn't neither. An' fur that I ..." He got no further. A shot aimed by a guard who had come on the scene unexpectedly struck him across the top of the head. He crashed on his face, completely stunned. For an instant there was a dead silence; then the men began to surge forward angrily. In that split second, however, de Brock also acted.

With a sudden tremendous surge he flung Jess from him and lashed out with his fist. The knife went flying. Another shot exploded and Jess heard the bullet whine past his ear. It was no time to argue, bereft as he was of his only weapon.

He hurled himself on to the high palings surrounding the yard and began to scramble up them. Another shot followed him but in the gloom the aim was poor. He scrambled clear, dropped to the other side of the fence, then began to run under the stars.

For a time he heard the explosion of guns, saw the flash of them in the darkness behind him. But they grew fainter as he went onwards across the pasture land. In every way he had the advantage now, the moonless night sheltering him. Bright though the starlight was it was not sufficient to reveal him against the dark of the greensward.

Once, perhaps an hour after he had escaped, a party of horsemen approached him, but he slipped into a fold of the land and remained until they had gone. Finally, at what he judged must be some time after midnight, he settled himself to sleep in an outcropping of manzanita, satisfied that nobody could approach without awakening him.

Exhausted as he was, sleep came readily, nor was he once disturbed.

In the cold air of the coming dawn he was on his way again, knee-deep in mist wreaths, his joints stiff from the exposure of the night. He hurried to restore his circulation, gradually finding himself becoming warmer and less cramped. At the first golden shafts of sun-up he paused to take his bearings.

He had come a long way during the dark hours. The Square-8 was still visible at the far end of the valley, a good four miles distant perhaps. Nearer to him, in the other direction, nestling at the foot of the mountain range, was another ranch, fairly large, but with none of the prosperous signs of de Brock's spread. Jess contemplated it, fingering his unshaven chin; then at last he made up his mind to risk it and started off through the grass at a loping run. He kept low down on the off chance that one or other of de Brock's gunhawks might be on the lookout for him, but nothing disturbed the mellow peace of the dawn.

As he came nearer the ranch he saw that big though the corrals were there were no more than half a dozen steers in them, and no signs of men working about the place, as there should have been at this hour on any normal spread. There was a forlorn, poverty-stricken look about the place which seemed to suggest that the ruthless hand of Wilton de Brock had already struck here.

Crossing the yard at a run so as not to attract undue attention, Jess came up to the porch and knocked sharply on the inner door, the screen-door being latched back to the wall. There was a long pause; then the door opened perhaps half an inch and a gun barrel projected at him. He gave a start as he saw it and raised his hands slowly.

"Get out of here, and quickly, if you don't want lead!" a girl's voice commanded. It was a voice with the culture of education, at least, sufficient to enable her to place her sentences correctly.

Jess kept his hands raised and tried to see who was back of the voice, but without success. The sun was not yet shining on this side of the ranch-house. There was only a dim, shadowy figure without a sign of outline.

"I'm unarmed," he said. "All I want is a meal, and that I can pay for. If you can provide it, even hand it through the door if you want, I'll be on my way. That's gospel truth, ma'm."

"Stop telling lies! You're one of de Brock's men spying out the place, and it's like your impudence to come right up to the porch to do it. Fortunately I saw you from the window as you crossed the yard. Now go, before I shoot you. I've no time for de Brock or any of the owl-hooters connected with him."

Jess glanced about him and then gave a start. In the far distance a lone rider was approaching, coming towards this very ranch. It could be one of de Brock's gunmen — "Quit fooling around!" Jess implored hoarsely, through the doorcrack. I'm on the level. I'm escaping from de Brock if you must have the truth."

"I don't believe — "

Jess did not waste any further time on words. Suddenly he slammed his foot against the base of the door and then jumped back. The gun exploded harmlessly but the door tore from its chain and swung wide. In one dive he was inside, wrenching the revolver from the girl who held it. Swinging back to the door he closed it and shot the bolts into place.

"All right, then, shoot!" the girl snapped.

Jess turned and looked at her in the dim light of the hall. He could see thick dark hair and the outline of a blue short-sleeved blouse and dark riding skirt. Then without further ceremony he took her shoulder and pushed her into the brighter light of the living room. It was sparsely furnished. Here again was the same air of poverty which had been noticeable outside.

"Shootin' down a woman will be just about your mark, I take it?" the girl asked, flinging back her head in contempt, defiance in her amber-coloured eyes. "You wouldn't be a true disciple of de Brock otherwise. Get on with it! I'm not afraid of you!"

Jess stood looking at her. She was not exactly beautiful, but she had clear, intelligent features, a strong mouth, and the firm lines of a girl accustomed to perpetual open air in these sundrenched wastes. At the moment the icy hatred with which her face was masked made Jess feel profoundly uncomfortable.

"How many times do I have to tell you I'm not a gunman?" he demanded.

"As many times as you like, and I still won't believe you. It's written all over you."

"Listen for a minute, gal, for heaven's sake!"

"Supposing I don't?"

"The name's Jess Burton. I've escaped from de Brock's ranch prison and I need help. Mebby this will convince you that I'm quite harmless."

Jess tossed the gun on the table. Something of the stony contempt left the girl's face at that; then both she and Jess turned sharply at a pounding on the porch door.

"That could be one of de Brock's men," Jess breathed, whipping the gun up again. "And if so it won't take me ten seconds to put him where — "

"No!" The girl shook her dark head quickly. "It'll be my father, I expect. He rode into Yellow Gulch and he's due back around now."

"Sure?"

"Sure as can be, yes."

"Okay, but just the same I'll stand here and watch."

The girl left the room with graceful swiftness and drew back the door bolts. A tall man in riding pants and dark shirt became visible, tugging off his broad-brimmed hat. Immediately he put a protective arm about the girl's shoulders as he saw Jess, stubbled and grim, standing with the gun in the doorway of the living room.

"It's all right, this is my father," the girl said. "You can put that gun down."

"Bolt the door again," Jess instructed. "In case of surprise visits from strangers."

The grey-haired man with the slope shoulders did so; then with a frown he came forward. His features were gaunt and sharply defined, but there was something handsome and distinguished about him.

"What's all this about?" he demanded. "What right have you to come gunnin' on my spread an' scare my gal here?"

Jess tossed the gun back onto the table and shrugged. His eyes met those of the elderly rancher steadily.

"I'm assumin' that you're friendly," he answered. "Automatically you should be if you're opposed to Wilton de Brock. I know your daughter is."

"So that's th' way of things." The tall, gaunt rancher still looked puzzled. "Where are you headed, stranger? Away from de Brock, or towards him?"

"In a sense, both," Jess answered. "I escaped from his ranch at the other end of the valley, but I don't aim to try an' escape any further. It's time somebody stayed put around here and figgered out where de Brock should be made to get off. I'm Jess Burton. I was just a plain hombre until de Brock as good as hijacked me into his outfit. I stayed one day and then quit — in my own way.

Right now I imagine de Brock's men will be out on the prod for me. I haven't seen any of 'em but that isn't any guarantee. Lead might start flyin' at any moment."

"Yore right about de Brock's men," the rancher confirmed. "On my way back from Yellow Gulch I saw quite a few gunnin' parties on the prod, but I didn't know what for. They didn't stop me, an' even if they had I couldn't ha' told 'em anythin', of course."

The rancher studied Jess intently for a while and then seemed to make up his mind.

"All right, Burton, I'll take a chance," he said. "My name is Calvert, Len Calvert. This is my daughter, Fay. We've bin livin' here for 'bout ten years now, ever since my wife died of a chill back in Kansas. Get some breakfast for us, Fay," Calvert added, and with a nod the girl went from the room.

Jess watched her go and then switched back to the rancher.

"Seems to me," Jess said, "that a man's treated like an escaped convict around here if he doesn't do just as de Brock tells him! Or anyways that's bin the set-up so far. I'm minded to make some big changes in the scheme of things."

"Yeah?" The rancher seemed to reflect over this.

"Thanks for trusting me," Jess added quietly, as he and Calvert settled in chairs at the table. "From the look of things around here you've as much grudge against de Brock as I have."

"Meanin'?"

"Your nearly empty corrals and the look of despair about the place. I noticed it straight away. Guess you can pretty well read a man's fortunes from the look of his cattle."

"Yeah, yore pretty well right."

Calvert brooded for a while, watching as his daughter returned and began to set out a breakfast for three.

"Yes, I suppose I do owe most of my troubles to de Brock," Calvert confirmed finally. "But just the same I'm a fatalist. I don't believe in fightin' the inevitable because I guess you get in a far worse mess that way. If a man's got the dice loaded against him he just can't win and it's suicide to try. An' so there it is."

Jess stared. "But, Mr Calvert, you can't mean that you agree with the things de Brock's doin' in this territory. No decent thinkin' man could."

"With most of my cattle stolen and my daughter and I livin' under th' threat of eviction? No! I don't agree with de Brock but I do believe it's safer sometimes to swim with th' current than against it. I'm no longer young enough to fight de Brock. So I leave him be. It's simpler that way, I reckon."

Fay put down the coffee jug irritably and gave Jess a very direct look.

"What my father really means is that he doesn't fight de Brock because he thinks things will be easier if he doesn't ."

"Fay!" her father protested sharply. The way you put it makes it sound really bad."

"It's meant to, dad!" The girl's amber-coloured eyes switched back to Jess. "I've tried to explain to him that that can only lead to disaster in the end, but he doesn't see it. Or else he *won't*!"

"Have it your own way, gal," Calvert said, shrugging, "but we're still here and de Brock's left us alone."

"Now that he's stolen everything we had, yes," the girl retorted, her eyes flaming. "Before de Brock came we had a prosperous spread and a nice cattle business. Now our steers have mysteriously vanished 'til we've only half a dozen left. We know who is to blame, but what's the good of that if we don't act?" Fay sighed and shook her head. "Even the boys have left us because there was no work for them to do. Now we're living on the money we made in the good days, but it can't last for ever. Next thing we know de Brock will swoop and throw us out. I'm expecting it at any moment, which is one reason why I thought you were an advance scout, or something, Mr Burton."

"You mean he'll *buy* us out," Calvert said. "And when he does we'll go."

Fay looked at him helplessly. "But, dad, de Brock doesn't *buy* what he wants: he takes. When he's good and ready we'll be thrown out, same as happened at the Crossed-J, the Leaning-9, and the 5-Circle."

"I'll defy any eviction order de Brock sees fit to issue!" Calvert retorted stubbornly.

"Some good it will do you," Fay snapped. "If we don't go we'll be hanged here on the property as a warning to others who might think of refusing. That's de Brock's technique. I tell you we've only two alternatives — either fight de Brock by gathering together the remaining homesteaders and arming ourselves for attack; or else report the whole business to the nearest State Governor. That's an angle I've been thinking about for some time."

"You'll take too big a risk reporting it to a Governor," Jess said quietly. "I know because I've been on th' inside an' I've heard how de Brock works. But you might stand a chance if you an' the remaining ranchers formed into a body for your own protection. In fact it seems t' me about the only course left open. How many do you think you could count on to lend a hand?"

"About fifty men and women," the girl replied. "And every one of them hating de Brock!"

"Good enough! As I figger it, de Brock has around twenty men who might be called his strong-arm squad.

That means that with fifty ranchers on our side we could
— "

"I'll have nothin' t' do with it!" Calvert interrupted angrily, banging his fist on the table. "You can do as you like, Burton, once yore on your way, but don't drag us into it. There ain't no call for you to come bustin' in here with a lot of bright ideas!"

"I'm entitled to speak for myself, anyways," Fay said sharply. "What's more, I'm going to!"

"I'm your father, gal, an' as long as I live you'll do as I say. I've got things figgered out to protect th' both of us, and I won't be a party to no range war, for that's what it'd come to. Once the shootin' starts anythin' can happen, and we can't possibly win with the power de Brock's got. I don't aim to take a long chance like that."

"You prefer, then, to sit and take what's coming to you?" Jess asked, tackling his meal.

"I've my own way of runnin' things," Calvert answered. "I've no objections to givin' you a meal an' th' chance to rest up a bit. But that's as far as it goes. An' even that's a risk I don't like takin'. If de Brock's men turn up and find you here I'm liable to get strung up an' you beside me, with mebby Fay thrown in as a makeweight."

"The moment I've finished this meal, for which I'll pay, I'll be on my way," Jess promised. "Forget everything else I said. I'll work things out for myself."

"How?" Fay persisted, ignoring her father's angry glance. "Just how? I really want to know."

"Well, there are about a dozen men back at the Square-8 who are willin' to throw in their lot with me and try and destroy de Brock's stranglehold on this territory. I aim to free them and then we'll work in our own way. Our job is to undo every wrong de Brock has committed and make him suffer into the bargain. When we have finally destroyed his power an' gotten all the evidence we need, we'll bring in a State Governor to look into things. That's the only way ever to get action around here."

"Then you're a danged fool!" Calvert declared, "de Brock'll shoot you outa hand the moment you expose yourself, and you know it!"

"*If* I expose myself," Jess corrected, getting to his feet. "I would have liked you on our side, Mr Calvert, an' your daughter, too. Since that can't be done I'll see how the other ranchers feel about it." He laid a ten dollar on the table. "That should cover the meal an' everythin'," he added. "And thanks again."

The die-hard rancher sat looking at him fixedly. "You're just a sucker for trouble, Burton, ain't you?" he asked. "I've never seen anybody quite like you."

"I know injustice when I see it, an' if it's humanly possible I aim to stop it. Since you won't be joinin' me personally there is one other thing you might do."

"Well?"

Jess nodded to the nickel-plated .45 on the table. "Let me have that to protect myself with. I can't buy it from you 'cos I haven't that much money. You've two guns in your belt there: you can surely spare that one?"

Calvert laid his big hand across it. "Sorry, Burton. If you want to go around killin' folk you must do it with your own hardware. I'm not bein' a party to anything aimed against de Brock."

"But, dad, that's absolutely ridiculous!" Fay protested. "After all that gun — "

"Be quiet, gal, an' let me handle things th' way I see best. This gun stays right where it is. I don't aim to have trouble stirred up in a land that's too full of it already."

Jess hesitated and then hunched a shoulder. "Okay, have it your own way. Thanks again. 'Bye, Miss Fay."

He turned and left, but he had hardly reached the base of the porch steps before the girl came hurrying after him. She caught his arm and stopped him, holding out the .45, butt foremost. He looked at it in surprise.

"Take it," Fay urged. "Heaven knows, you need it."

"I sure do, Miss Fay, but what about your pop? He was mighty positive about me not havin' it."

"It's my gun, not his. I can do what I like with my own property, after all."

Jess studied her, her earnest amber eyes, her wealth of dark hair flowing in the soft breeze. For a moment he compared her to the shadowy creature who had ordered him away not an hour before.

"I can't figure out how a man like your pop comes to have a daughter like you," he said. "You've twice his spirit. Mebby I'd work it out better if I'd known your Ma."

"You don't want to pay too much heed to what dad says," the girl answered. "He's acting as he thinks best, I suppose, trying to protect me in his way by not causing de Brock any trouble. But I don't mind trouble if only we have justice, and that's why I'm with you in your plans even though at this stage I daren't join you personally. My father's religious," she added, as though that explained everything.

"Y'mean that 'turn the other cheek' stuff?"

"You might call it that. Makes him seem cowardly but he isn't really."

Jess smiled. "Thanks for the gun. As for the religious angle, I've nothin' against it. But it doesn't seem such a powerful weapon in a region like this."

Fay changed the subject before he could proceed any further.

"You'll need a horse, won't you?" she questioned.

"It'd help a lot, yes. My own's back at the Square-8 and I ain't sure I'll ever see it again. But yore takin' a big risk lettin' me have a mount, aren't you?"

"Too big a risk!" Calvert himself declared, from the porch. "Come back here, gal, whilst you're safe. You've done enough damage as it is givin' your gun to this hombre."

"He can have my own mare," Fay retorted defiantly. "If you won't help a man to get action, dad, then I will! That, to my way of thinking, is only downright common sense."

Deliberately she turned her back to him and led the way to a stable at the side of the ranch-house. Jess half followed her, then stood waiting, one eye cocked on the silent rancher as he watched stonily. Presently the girl reappeared, leading a frisky and saddled chestnut mare.

"Save you a lot of walking," she said, giving the reins into Jess' hand. "You can return her sometime if you ever get your own horse back."

"I'll come and see you again in any case," Jess promised, vaulting into the saddle after he had shaken the girl's hand firmly. "An' thanks a lot for the help.

You'll be hearin' plenty about me before yore much older, I reckon."

Spurring the mare forward he cantered across the yard, waving as he went. The girl responded, but not her father. He remained like a statue on the porch, watching, and Jess could imagine the brooding stare in those eyes.

Then he turned his attention to his own safety. To be on the alert for sudden trouble was essential. At any moment hidden gunmen from the Square-8 might appear, and there was little doubt in Jess' mind but what they'd shoot first and ask questions afterwards. So he turned to the only spot where he could feel reasonably safe. The mountain range.

Here he remained throughout the torrid day, feeding on the few roots and edible berries he found, and slaking his and the mare's thirst from the mountain stream. Then at — nightfall — he prepared for action. He checked over the gun the girl had given him. There were six bullets in it, not many if it came to desperate fighting, but enough to get by perhaps. He decided that the sooner he obtained a gun-belt of .45 cartridges the better he'd feel.

It was completely dark when he left his cave hideout, speeding down the mountain trail which presently became an arroyo stretching away under the stars like a pale grey line amidst the grasslands. With the night wind rushing in his face he rode swiftly along the valley side, his gun ready for instant action, his destination the Square-8.

He reached it in half an hour and then began to ride more warily. A quarter of a mile from it he slipped from the mare, tethered her securely to a thicket, and finished his trip on foot. His eyes were fixed on the lights of the bunkhouse and the glow from the curtained windows of the ranch itself.

When he reached the high paling fence which completely enclosed the ranch yard, he paused and looked about him. There was no sign of any sentries on duty, unless it was that his crouching advance had been stealthy enough to enable him to elude them. With a swift jump he gripped the top of the fence and hauled himself up. On the other side, a few yards away, a gunman lounged. He was in the shadows cast by the kerosene lamps hanging outside the ranch-house. His task, apparently, was not so much to stop anybody coming in as to prevent any of the hijacked outfit getting out.

Jess grinned to himself, poising his lithe body for a moment. Then he leapt. He landed on top of the gunman before he had the least chance to protest or cry out. A violent blow on the back of the neck with the gun butt silenced him completely.

Glancing about him as he worked, Jess took the man's gun and cartridge belt, strapping it about his own waist; then he glided towards the bunk-house. The doorway was open, pale kerosene glow streaming from within the low-roofed building. There came the low murmuring of men's voices.

Cautiously Jess peered round the door edge into the dreary building. There were perhaps twelve cowpunchers present, and the reason for their quiet behaviour and muttered tones became immediately obvious. Seated facing them, his back to the door, was one of de Brock's guards, a rifle across his knees, a cigarette dangling from the corner of his heavy-lipped mouth.

Jess studied the scene more intently. The men present were chiefly those who had vowed they would not join in any attempted getaway. Those who had been willing to take a chance, including Ox himself, were absent. Jess wondered why, and his lips tightened as he speculated on whether or not they had been shot for their mutinous behaviour.

He came to a snap decision and acted. Leaping forward he had his forearm under the guard's chin and was holding him in an immovable grip before the man could make a move to save himself. He struggled futilely, his hands flailing, but he could not dislodge the grip Jess had on him. The assembly of men watched grim-faced. None made a move to interfere.

"A little information is all I need from you, my friend," Jess breathed, snatching the man's cigarette from his lips. Then to the assembly he added, "And if any of you guys feel like changin' your minds and clearin' out now's your chance! I ain't likely to come again. Or are all of you the yellow-bellies you seem to be?"

The men looked at each other, waverers most of them, but they remained still.

"They got more sense 'n risk floggin', or death — or worse," the guard panted, fighting to free himself. "An' you'll never git outa this alive either, Burton. Yuh must be plain crazy even to think yuh can."

"Yeah? We'll see … Now you can start tellin' me somethin'. Where's Ox an' the rest of the boys who were willin' to back him an' me in a getaway?"

"Why in tarnation should I tell yuh that?"

"Because I want to know — and I can be mighty persuasive when the mood seizes me."

"If yuh think that scares me, Burton, yuh'd best start figgerin' out a new line."

Very deliberately Jess blew the ash from the cigarette he was holding, then he moved it slowly downwards towards the guard's upturned face. As he saw it coming straight for his left eye he thrashed and heaved mightily, but the armlock was too much for him. The glowing point of the weed came at him relentlessly.

"Okay, okay. Wait!" he panted, sweating. "I tell yuh what yuh want to know. They got solitary fur what they did. Ox an' the rest uv them."

"An' where's solitary?" Jess snapped. "Hurry it up! I can't hang around here all night."

"In — in the yard. There's a flagstone in the middle of it, with an iron ring. Ox an' th' others is below. Bin there for some time."

"All right, take me to them." Jess dug his .45 in the man's back as he released his hold on his neck. "If you say one word outa turn, God help you!"

The guard got up slowly, hesitated, and then began to move to the doorway. He had sense enough to realize that he stood no chance and that if need be Jess would shoot to kill. His hands slightly raised he walked out of the bunkhouse and across the yard in the kerosene glow.

Jess followed steadily, his eyes darting about for any fresh guards who might appear. Evidently, though, with the bunkhouse under supervision, the guards were not over-zealous, for nothing was seen of them.

Reaching the flagstone the puncher nodded to it. Through the iron ring in its centre was padlocked an iron bar. Jess stood looking down at it for a moment.

"Get it up!" he ordered.

"It's a two-man job."

"Shut up and get busy. A big lunkhead like you shouldn't need any help."

The man scowled, unfastened the padlock with a key from his pocket, and flung the iron bar aside. Then he heaved the flat stone away. From the pit below there came the sound of voices. Jess stepped to the hole, never once removing his eyes from the guard.

"You fellers down there!" he called, not raising his voice too much in case it carried. "It's safe to come up. Make it quick!"

There was the sound of scrambling and excited conversation from the depths. Then, shoved from beneath, Ox made his appearance over the edge of the cavity, his ugly face emerging into the yellow light.

"Jess!" he gasped, staring. "Say, is this somethin'! We figgered you'd run out on us."

"Then start figgering again, Ox. I was only bidin' my time."

Ox hauled himself out and moved to Jess' side, but when he began talking Jess waved him away.

"Save it, Ox. I've my work cut out watching this guy here. How many are there below?"

"Six — packed tight. They'll be up pronto."

They were, scrambling quickly over the stone rim into the yard. All of them were dirty, unshaven, haggard after their ordeal below.

"This skunk had as much t'do with it as anybody," Ox breathed, clenching his enormous fists and moving towards the guard. "It wus him who kicked us below — an' I mean kicked! de Brock figgered on leavin' us here — 'til we rotted, I guess, which we should ha' done but fur you, Jess. I guess there oughta be some kind uv reply to that sorta thing."

"Mebby there is, but we haven't time for it now," Jess said. "We're leavin' here, all of us. Put that skunk below. Best place for him."

"Pleasure!" Ox grinned, and his big left hand flashed out with the impact of a steam piston.

The guard absorbed the blow across his face and keeled over backwards. A further terrific punch to the base of the skull sent him crashing head first into the cavity. With supreme ease Ox lifted the stone and dropped it back into position, snapping the padlock firmly. A wide grin had spread across his ugly face as he looked at Jess again.

"Now what?" he questioned.

"You okay?" Jess asked him. "Last I saw of you you'd been creased by a bullet."

"That? Huh! Just parted me hair, that's all. I think we oughta go now an' give that mug de Brock what's bin owin' to him fur far too long. He spends too much time talkin' fancy an' doin' as he likes. A mug like that wants payin' back in his own coin."

"Later mebby," Jess said. "Not now."

"Why in hell not! I'm gettin' sick uv takin' on th' lamp fur that guy! He's unprepared an — "

"I said later!" Jess snapped. "Never kill a man whilst you can make use of him. Around here, Ox, I'm runnin' things. An' see that you get it through your thick skull. I've freed you and these other fellers for only one reason, so's you can have a chance to fight back, but under my orders. Any objections?"

The other men were silent as Jess looked at them questioningly.

Ox hesitated, then shook his bullet head. "Okay, Jess, have it your way. But we ain't goin' to get far unarmed. This place is lousy with gunmen, or I don't know de Brock."

"Just what I was thinkin', but it seems to me that a man who does as much shootin' and pillagin' around the territory as de Brock does must have an armoury somewheres from which we can take our pick of weapons. I aim to find it whilst we're here and make a selection."

"That'll take some doin', Jess!" Shorty protested. "Sounds like walkin' right into the enemy camp to me!"

Jess grinned. "Mebby it is. But if de Brock himself tells us where the armoury is we oughta get some place. Let's see what he has to say for himself."

3. Tough Hombres

Inwardly astonished at Jess' audacity, but quite willing to follow his lead, the men trailed behind him up to the ranch-house. He ignored the porch, walking instead to the lighted but curtained floor-to-ceiling window facing the barns and outhouses. Hurling his shoulder against the flimsy frame he tumbled into the living room beyond, bringing up sharp and firing his gun.

He was just in time. In the split second of warning de Brock seated with his wife at a well-laid table, had whipped out his Colt. It spun out of his hand and clattered uselessly into the fire grate. He sat glaring, his fingers tingling, as Jess walked slowly into the room with his grim-faced cohorts behind him.

"Okay, de Brock, so yore surprised," Jess said calmly, a glint in his eyes. "That's how I meant it to be. An' before I'm through mebby you'll be surprised a lot more." "Now you've had your surprise," de Brock grated, "what more do you want?"

"Plenty! But I'll come to it in my own time. Do you good to wait a bit and give somebody else a chance. Okay, boys," Jess added, after an interval which he had made as long as possible. "Help yourselves to food and drink. It's time you had some at de Brock's expense."

The cattle baron remained silent, exchanging glances with his wife as the food and drink on the table was wolfed, Jess too satisfying his gnawing appetite. Then presently he said:

"Remember what I told you last night? That I was goin' to let you live so's you'd take longer to die?"

"You'll never get off this spread alive, any of you!" de Brock vowed breathing hard. "As for you, Burton, and your fool warnings, I don't give a rap if you try to — "

"Shut up an' get on your feet!"

"I'll be — "

Jess fired for the second time and the bullet tore the table-cloth in a smoking line not an inch from the cattle baron's hand. He got up, making a tremendous effort to control his fury. His wife sat on, glancing from one to the other.

"Keep a watch outside, Ox," Jess ordered, without turning. "This gun of mine may bring some of the jackals around to see what gives. Now, de Brock, where do you keep your guns and ammo?"

"That's my business!"

"Mine, too. Start talkin'!"

"To a saddle tramp like you? What the hell do you think I am?"

"Better not be too obstinate, de Brock. I'll give you five seconds to answer my question."

The cattle baron remained silent, his powerful mouth set. Jess eyed him stonily and counted five; then he called Shorty over to him.

"Yeah, Jess?" Shorty asked.

"Put the poker in the fire there an' hot it up with the bellows. When it's good and red see how Mrs de Brock will enjoy havin' her face branded like a steer! Without bein' disrespectful to Mrs de Brock, she ain't exactly beautiful anyways, so mebby a little brandin' will hardly be noticed." Shorty blinked a little. You're kiddin',

Jess?" "Do as yore told," Jess ordered implacably, and the little cowpuncher scuttled to obey the instruction even if he could hardly believe his ears.

Mrs de Brock shifted uncomfortably in her chair, emotion showing for the first time in her square features. Her husband looked at her, then his pale, steely eyes fastened sharply on Jess.

"Pretty low down kind of fighter, aren't you?" he asked grimly. "Branding a woman to get information from her husband! I thought of several things you might do, Burton, but never this!"

"Now you know different," Jess said calmly.

"Dragging a woman into it and making her squirm is low tactics, Burton."

"Her husband can prevent it," Jess replied tersely. "And I guess that if you wanted somethin' real badly, de Brock, you wouldn't stop at brandin' a woman either. Yore not the only guy around here who can be tough."

Jess waited, his face murderous in its intentness, his gun rock-steady.

There was a long, grim pause: it was broken by Ox poking his head round the shattered window.

"Two guards so fur, Jess," he announced. "They're out cold. Yore in th' clear fur the moment. If any more come along I'll break their blasted heads ag'inst each other!"

"Okay, Ox, stay on guard. What about that iron, Shorty? Takin' a long time, isn't it?"

"Yeah, Jess, sure is, but I reckon it's good an' red now, like yuh wanted it."

Shorty pulled the iron out of the grate, holding the handle in his folded kerchief. He stopped when he came in front of Mrs de Brock and she shrank back in her

46

chair. Shorty licked his lips, hesitated, then lowered the iron slightly.

"Guess I ain't got th' guts to do this," he muttered. "Durn me, Jess, it's more'n I can take!"

"Gettin' soft, huh?" Jess took the poker in his free hand and stood ready for action. He advanced the poker steadily in an unshaken hand towards the woman's terrified face — then to his infinite relief de Brock stopped him.

"Just a minute, Burton, take it easy. I'll tell you what you want to know. I can see when I'm cornered."

"'bout time," Jess growled, flinging the poker into the grate with a nerve-jarring clatter. "All right, where's the armoury? An' if you play any tricks, de Brock, I'll let you have it here an' now and let the future take care of itself."

The cattle baron jerked his head and led the way into an adjoining room. Jess and the other men followed him — but not Ox. He stayed behind to keep guard over the living room and the rancher's wife. Crossing to a big wall cupboard de Brock unfastened the doors and revealed the rifles, revolvers, and ammunition within.

"Very pretty," Jess commented, giving him a grim look.

"All nicely loaded up to start a range war, huh? Nothin' like bein' prepared in advance."

"I intend finally to rule this territory in its entirety, Burton, and in the process I'll grind you to powder and all these louts who trail around with you. You have me at the pistol point now, but it won't always be so. The moment I'm free to act things will happen such as you'd never thought possible."

"Yeah? Take care it isn't the other way round! You're not idiot enough to think you can cross swords with me and get away with it, are you?"

Jess said nothing further. He helped himself to a .45 complete with loaded gun belt, then motioned to his men to choose their own weapons. This done he led the way back into the living room and sent Ox to make his selection. He returned with twin .38s strapped to his heavy thighs.

"I guess I feel properly dressed with th' hardware back in place," he commented. "But jus' the same, if things get too awkward I've a pair of mansized fists I can use. All I need is a face 'bout th' size uv de Brock's to plant 'em in!"

"Understand this, de Brock," Jess said levelly, his gun still pointed. "We're not thieves."

"You're not? It would be interesting to know what you do call yourselves!"

"We're takin' what is due to us, even though it may not be the original article!" Jess snapped. "From each of us you took guns and cartridges: we're taking 'em back. It will be kinda poetic to hound you down with your own weapons every time you make a move."

de Brock smiled coldly. "You're fool enough to think you can get away with that?"

"You'll see. I'm warnin' you, de Brock. Stay within limits an' run things in a proper way and you'll be okay. I don't consider it my business to worry over things you may have done before I got into this territory. But I shall worry over what you do from now on."

"Oh, you will? Is that supposed to make me quake with terror, or something?"

"Nope. Just plain words, that's all. If you dare to lay a hand on any of the settlers around here you'll pay for it to the limit. That's a promise. In any event, whether you attack any more settlers or not I'm going to ruin your empire for you because it's too dangerous to be left standin'. I'll do it if it takes me the rest of my life!"

"You'll have to act fast then, Burton, because I have the impression your life hasn't much longer to run, at least, not if I have anything to do with it."

Jess ignored the threat. "You also took horses from each of us," he said. "We'll take one each as we leave — and you'll see that we leave safely. Now get moving to the stables. You too, Mrs de Brock. We're not leaving you behind to raise the alarm."

The cattle baron shrugged and led the way outside through the window. Two guards who had just come up immediately trained their guns, then hesitated as de Brock raised his hand. He looked at them grimly, but there was nothing he could do. "Take it easy, boys," he ordered. "No shooting." They relaxed, compelled to stand watching as all but Jess selected the mounts they fancied, saddled them, and then led them into the yard.

"Which about completes this evening's business," Jess said. "But I don't guarantee but what we'll be back some other evening. I already have a mare so I don't need a mount."

"Where did you get it?" de Brock demanded, frowning. "Stole it, I suppose?"

Jess only grinned enigmatically and motioned his men towards the gates. He kept de Brock covered until he could no longer hold it. Then he leapt on the back of Ox's saddle and the entire party sped off quickly under the stars. Reaching his own tethered mare Jess jumped down, went over to the animal and swung into the saddle, following his comrades as they raced across the starlit pastureland. In a while he caught up with Ox.

"Where are we headin'?" Ox demanded. "You got that figgered out 'mongst other things? Ain't much use in us just goin' any place. These things want organisin'."

You don't have to tell me," Jess retorted. "We're goin' to the mountains. I've a cave up there. But we're not goin' there direct 'cos we need food, and that includes fodder for th' animals if we're to survive. That bein' so we're goin' to town and the general stores."

"Raid the joint, y'mean?" Ox grinned. "That suits me fine! For the fust time, Jess, yuh's started talkin' in my language. Take what we like an — "

"We'll pay for what we get," Jess interrupted. "Get it straight, Ox, that we're not outlaws pilfering as we choose. We'd be no better'n de Brock if we behaved like that. We're goin' to see that there's justice in this valley until we've swept it clean of the stink of that polecat, an' ranchers can breathe free an' easy an' know they're safe. Got that?"

Ox rode on in silence for a while before he answered. His slow-moving brain took a long time to work things out.

"Yeah, I get it," he assented finally. "But I don't see how this small lot uv us is goin' to defeat de Brock. Seems t'me it's a short life an' a merry one 'til we're beaten. Why not make it good an excitin' an' do what we want where we want? I never could see any sense in pullin' yuh punches when there ain't any real need."

"Step out of line, Ox, and I'll finish you," Jess warned him. "That's a threat, an' I mean it. I want you for a trusted henchman, but if you go against th' stream don't be surprised if you drown in it."

"Okay, okay, yuh don't have ta get tough about it. But tell me one thing, where's th' money comin' from to pay fur th' food an' stuff we'll need? Or mebby yore so busy bein' a saint yuh haven't given it a thought!"

"I can tell you right now who's payin' for things," Jess answered dryly. "Shorty."

"Huh?" Shorty squeaked, a little way ahead, hipping round in his saddle. "Why me?"

"Better hand it over, Shorty," Jess advised. "If you thought I didn't see you pick up that roll of notes lyin' on th' mantelshelf in de Brock's livin' room, yore crazy! I've told you before about bein' too light-fingered, but this time it's a help. No reason why de Brock shouldn't finance his enemies. God knows, he's stolen enough stuff himself. I s'pose you thought you'd keep that wad to yourself, huh? Sorry, but it doesn't work that way when we're desperate."

"But Jess, look-ee here — "

Shorty's protest was cut short. "Give, feller, all of it! Y'know better'n to argue when my mind's made up."

Shorty felt in his hip pocket and handed over a wad of notes as Jess came riding up beside him. With one hand he flipped the corners and peered at the bundle in the starlight.

"Hundred-dollar bills!" he commented. "Must be pretty nearly forty of 'em here. Four thousand dollars'll finance the campaign very nicely."

"Are yuh aimin' to tell us that we don't share an' share alike?" Ox asked grimly.

"Not while I'm in charge. But I don't see that a hundred apiece should hurt you," Jess added. "Sort of initiation fee."

He pulled out the necessary separate $100 bills as he rode and handed them over. All the men appeared satisfied, except Ox. He muttered a surly thanks and said no more. Jess passed no remark either but he did wonder what was going on in the big cowpuncher's brutish, slow-witted brain.

The General Stores was closed when they hit town, but under Jess' imperious hammering on the double doors it did not stay closed for long. The little, bald-headed storekeeper was all set to protest vehemently at this sudden invasion after business hours, but he changed his mind as Jess' gun prodded him in the stomach.

"What is this?" the storekeeper demanded, pop-eyed. A hold up or sump'n?"

"Nope, official business. Say nothin' an' you won't get hurt. And you'll get paid, Baldy. The gun's to make sure you open the shop specially for us, see?"

The little man backed into the dim expanse of the store, then at Jess' instructions he lighted the oil lamps. Jess cuffed up his hat on to his forehead and looked about him.

"Yeah, everythin' we need," he decided. "Bedrolls, food, razors, horse fodder, the works." Then he went into an itemised list of requirements, insisting on each man paying for his own necessities out of his hundred-dollar bill.

"Which I don't call fair!" Ox objected, as the storekeeper began to parcel up the provisions in cardboard containers. "Yuh know how much I got left outa that hundred smackers? Twenty! Twenty! What kind uv checken feed is that fur a man?"

"All you'll need," Jess told him. "The kind of life we're goin' to lead you won't need any more money than that."

"If it's all th' same to you, feller, I likes a drink now an ag'in!" Ox snapped. "Twenty dollars sure won't get me much firewater."

Jess looked at him steadily. "Whilst you work with me, Ox, you'll keep a clear head. The drinking's out. You seem to forget that de Brock will leave nothing unturned to get us. We can't afford to be pickled when that happens."

"I'm willin' t' risk it," Ox growled.

"What yore willin' t' do doesn't count. I'm thinkin' for the good uv the lot of us. An' don't try my patience too much, damn you!"

Ox gave a suspicious leer and licked his heavy lips.

"What about th' rest uv that cash you've stored away? Figgerin' on runnin' out with it?"

Jess tightened his lips and said nothing. Ox, too, seemed to realize he was saying too much in front of the storekeeper so he kept quiet thereafter until everything had been transported outside. Then when the men were all astride their mounts he began again:

"I don't reckon that it's right to ask a man t' follow yuh into heck knows what without even a drink!" he protested. "My throat's burnin' fit to crack it wide open."

"Mebbe yore right," Jess grinned. "I'm pretty caked up with dust in the throat myself. 'Sides, I've somethin' to say to the folks of this town, and there's no better place than th' Trail's End Saloon. Let's go."

"Now yore talkin'!" Ox cried, and spurred his horse forward. "Guess I had yuh figgered wrong, Jess."

Outside the saloon they dropped from their mounts and hitched the reins on the tie-rack.

"Not you," Jess said, pulling Shorty back as he waddled towards the boardwalk steps. "Watch these cayuses. There's plenty of stuff on them we can't afford to lose. You can go in when we come out."

Though grumbling, Shorty nevertheless obeyed, returning mournfully to his horse where he sat surveying the practically empty high street in the glow of kerosene light. The Trail's End, however, was anything but deserted. It was jammed full of cowpokes, cattle traders, half-breeds, Mexicans, and saddle-tramps, most of them keeping company with women. The air was thick with tobacco fumes and the gambling tables were busy. In a group Jess and his boys moved languidly across to the bar counter.

"Whisky," Jess told the barkeep, and then looked about him, his right hand resting lightly on his gun.

"I reckon this drink's necessary," Ox murmured to him, his eyes darting about the smoky expanse. "But I guess we're also stickin' our chins out, somethin' I never thought of. That's th' wust of me, I guess. I can never seem t' plan anything properly. Only knows what I want an' does it. But you've got a head on yuh an' should ha' thought uv it. If any uv de Brock's boys are around here they'll recognize us an' then there'll be trouble."

54

"There'll be trouble in any case," Jess told him. "Might as well be in here as any place else. From now on de Brock's got to realize that he's up against men as tough as himself. If he doesn't it'll be up to us to prove it to him."

Ox nodded and turned to his drink. He tossed it off and ordered another. Jess had just finished and started on the second when he found himself looking at a big man with a star badge on his shirt.

"I'd like a word with you guys," he said briefly "An' I mean all of you."

"Say on," Jess invited, "though I don't get the impression it'll be of any partic'lar interest to us."

"How do you know when I haven't told yuh anythin' yet?"

"I know that you only act under the orders of de Brock. That's sufficient, isn't it?"

Sheriff Hardacre's face became a deeper colour. "Mebby I do take orders from de Brock, but since he's the nateral boss around this region that's only sensible, ain't it?"

"I don't think so," Jess told him. "A sheriff's job is to dispense justice, not to be a hired stooge. It's a pity a few of the honest men around here don't shoot the tar outa you!"

"Why, you — "

"Hold it, sheriff!" Jess' gun leapt into his hand. "If you pull a rod on me I'll let you have it. Make no mistake about that. In the ordinary way I can be as kid-gloved as anybody, but around this territory things just ain't ordinary. You can only live if yore faster on the draw than the next guy. If yore minded to see if I'm faster than you with this hair-trigger, I'm ready an' waitin'."

The sheriff hesitated but he did not draw his gun. Jess gave a grim smile.

"Okay," he said briefly. "Now say what you've got t'say."

"I was goin' to tell you that the sooner you get outa here the better." Hardacre snapped. "There's trouble enough in this region without a bunch of hoodlums like you an' yore owl-hooters makin' things worse by crossin' de Brock."

"Thanks for the compliment," Jess said sourly. "How come you've sized us up as a bunch of hoodlums? Looks ain't everythin', y'know."

"I said hoodlums, an' I mean it! I know each one of you by sight 'cos I saw you at work on de Brock's spread when I called on him. It ain't healthy to do things around here which de Brock doesn't order."

Jess grinned, his revolver motionless.

"Speak your piece like a blasted parrot, don't you?" he asked. "My boys an' me are leavin' here when we get good and ready, but not 'til then. What d'you think you can do about it?"

"There's plenty of men in here who feel as I do; they'll shift you quick enough."

"Yeah?"

The sheriff looked about him upon the now silent, smoke-filled room. The men and women were watching, even if they were not taking decisive action. Jess waited, then he relaxed a little more comfortably, one elbow on the counter.

"We're ready for anythin' anybody likes to try," he said. "Don't forget what I told you about anybody who can shoot faster than I can. Come to think of it, I'm glad I met up with you, sheriff, because it decides me that yore another who'll have to be put out of office. A man like you who obeys another man instead of ordinary law ain't fit to be a sheriff. Am I right, folks?"

At the question flung at them, the men and women exchanged looks with each other, hesitating. Then one man rose, a bearded, bronzed fellow, well past middle age and plainly one of the valley settlers.

"Since th' rest uv you is scared t' talk while one man fights for the rest with his gun, I'll speak for you," he said.

"Good!" Jess approved, nodding. "Speak on, old timer, an' don't be scared of these lily-whites. I've got a bead on 'em an' they know it!"

"Yes, stranger, yore right," the rancher asserted. "There's never been any justice in this territory since de Brock took over. How can yuh get it with a crooked mayor an' sheriff? Yuh just can't —"

Sheriff Hardacre wheeled, his face bleak with murderous rage. In a split second he had his gun from its holster and fired point blank. The rancher hesitated, felt at his chest, and looked bewildered. Then he crashed heavily forward across the table in front of him.

"Reach!" Jess ordered, his gun jabbing in the sheriff's back.

The sheriff swung, ignoring the command, his gun flashing round. Jess fired remorselessly. The sheriff dropped his weapon, doubled up, then his knees buckled beneath him. He flattened on the floor, his flailing arm striking a cuspidor. It rolled away drunkenly and came to rest with a clang. There was silence and the stench of cordite fumes.

"I reckon he asked for that," Jess said grimly, looking about him. "In plain sight of all of you he shot down that rancher 'cos he dared raise his voice against de Brock. The sheriff got paid back and no misses. Okay?" he continued, his jaw tightening, "mebby it'll serve as an example far more than any words of mine could do. I came in here to tell you that from now on de Brock is going to find his control over this territory breakin' down. Those of you who believe in him will go with him to disaster: those of you who don't will find friends in me an' my boys. Reckon that puts the case clearly, doesn't it?"

The direct, ruthless methods of this young, unsmiling man with the power-packed body were something the assembled men and women hadn't seen in Yellow Gulch for many a long day. They looked first at Jess, then at the bodies of the rancher and the sheriff. Nobody said anything: the shadowy menace of Wilton de Brock's vengeance still made them consider it safer to keep quiet. Yet there was a murmuring amongst themselves as they exchanged opinions without openly declaring them.

"You'll be needin' a new sheriff," Jess said, stooping and whipping the sheriff's star from his shirt. "I might even take it on myself when I've finished cleanin' up. I'll keep this badge against the day that happens."

"Which is going to be a long time coming, Burton," a well educated voice commented from the batwings. "I think your trouble is that you are a little too impetuous."

Jess pivoted, his gun ready. At the same instant a revolver spat from the doorway, whipping the gun from his fingers. Wilton de Brock, impeccably dressed in a lounge suit, no hat on his shaven head, grinned round the smoke of his pearl-handled. 45.

4. Fire and Murder

"Just a little return for your visit to me at my ranch," he explained, coming forward. "Did it make your fingers sting, my friend? If so, my apologies. I suppose I might call it a little preliminary unpleasantness towards you before the big event, eh?"

Jess waited, his eyes narrowed, Ox and his men behind him. de Brock advanced with easy movements, stopping when he was within a yard of Jess.

"In regard to you, Burton, let me remind you of the old saying, 'a short life and a merry one'," he commented. "I'll be sorry to kill you, of course, because up to now I have quite enjoyed your fire and spirit. Were you to go on living you might become an enemy really worthy of watching, which is one obligation I do not intend to assume."

"Make sure you're not talkin' outa turn, de Brock," Jess breathed. "We've all got to die some day, an' some of us quicker than others, 'specially in this region."

"I always make sure, Burton; that is why I have so much power around here."

"You'd be more to the point if you said you couldn't help but be sure with nobody havin' th' guts to stand up to you. I've caught you out before today, de Brock, an' I aim to do it plenty more times yet."

"I notice," the cattle baron commented, "that you have already started your campaign of terror."

He considered the dead sheriff and the more distant figure of the sprawled rancher.

"Your hired jackal of a sheriff shot that rancher dead. So I shot the sheriff," Jess explained. "Seemed quite logical t' my way of thinkin'. When a man shoots another because he speaks the truth it's time he had some overdue lead comin' to him. I call that justice."

"From your way of thinking I suppose it was," de Brock agreed calmly, motioning the pop-eyed barkeep to hand him a drink. "But, of course, Burton, it just can't go on."

"No?" Jess eyed him narrowly.

"No!" de Brock swallowed some of his drink and continued, "Fortunately you are as big a fool as the rest of thos⟨ who have tried to cross me. Instead of making good your escape with these assassins of yours you had to come right here into the very heart of the town and brag about your exploits. I hardly thought you'd be such a damned fool.

However, when my look-outs reported that that was what you had done I decided I'd better come over. And here you all are, in a bunch." Cold lights glimmered in de Brock's pale eyes. "Makes it simple, does it not?"

"Mebby ... " Without any show of emotion Jess swallowed down the dregs of his second drink and put the glass back on the counter. He could hear Ox breathing heavily behind him and needed no imagination to guess that those massive fists were clenched.

"In regard to the murder of Sheriff Hardacre," the cattle baron continued, "I have since equalled the score."

Jess' eyes sharpened. "How?"

"You left that idiot Shorty Pearson on guard outside. I slugged him from behind with my Colt. Unfortunately, he had a thin skull ... You'll find his body lying under

61

the porch. I had my men put it there to save making the main street untidy."

"Yuh killed him?" Ox demanded fiercely. "Just like that? Fur nothin' at all?"

De Brock nodded looking surprised. "Why not? One less hoodlum to bother about. Now I shall have to take care of you gentlemen and with you out of my way I can move a little more freely But first, Burton, I'll trouble you for that sheriff's badge. You will never need it, whereas I shall have the mayor put it on a new law officer, one, I trust, with less inclination to open his mouth too wide. You see, I do agree with you in one respect, that Hardacre talked a lot more than was necessary. Discretion, I suppose, should be a sheriff's chief virtue."

Jess did not respond. He turned to the bar, facing it so that he could see everything in the back-bar mirrors. It gave him a chance to sum things up without the movement of his eyes being obvious.

"Hurry it up!" de Brock snapped. "I'm not going to stand here indefinitely waiting for that badge."

Jess still looked into the mirrors, satisfying himself that directly overhead there hung one of the kerosene lamps. The rest of his plan would depend on split-second timing.

"Okay," he said casually, feeling in his shirt with his left hand. Then with his right he suddenly whirled up the whisky bottle standing near de Brock's elbow and flung it unerringly at the lamp overhead. It went out in a splintering of glass and gushing of blazing oil.

Unprepared, de Brock dodged as glass pelted on him, then a ramrod fist struck him on the mouth with crashing force. He jolted backwards, his head and shoulders falling into piled-up bottles at the end of the counter. Helpless, he sagged to his knees. The entire sequence took perhaps five seconds and in that time Jess leapt from his position, dodging the bullets which exploded at him. His own guns in his hands, again he fired savagely, fighting his way to the nearest table. Upending it he jumped behind it for protection, Ox following immediately after him.

Pandemonium struck the saloon as the shots were exchanged. The men and women whirled and scuttled and fled through the bat-wings. The barkeep dodged behind his counter and stayed there. The big mirror splintered in the hail of lead which de Brock's trigger-men let loose.

De Brock himself, his upper lip bleeding profusely, remained crouched by the counter for a moment. Then he worked his way to the end of it and remained there, sniping at intervals, ducking back as woodwork splintered close to his face.

"Kill those other lamps, Ox," Jess murmured. Tut the place in darkness an' then we'll beat it. We can't get away with it otherwise."

"Okay, but it seems a pity t'go just when we wus gettin' warmed up."

Ox twisted round and sighted on the nearest lamp. It exploded in a clink of glass as he fired and the ignited oil spattered on the floor. The remaining and final lamp followed it and more blazing oil dropped. Jess watched it for a moment.

"Quick!" he breathed. "Let's get outa here before the place catches fire!"

To give the order was one thing, to put it into force another. The flames of the shattered lamps were already taking a firm hold on the dry wooden flooring. Apart from the danger of a conflagration the light was a give-away and made Jess, Ox, and those who crept with them, a constant target for the bullets ripping across the saloon.

But finally they reached the bat-wings and so as not to make themselves too noticeable they slid underneath them to prevent them swinging. Outside, three of de Brock's men were waiting on horseback. Taking no chances Jess and Ox fired at them simultaneously. Given no time to take aim the three men reeled from their saddles into the dust of the high street.

"Guess de Brock was right about Shorty," Jess said grimly, looking about him. "No sign of him anywhere but his horse is still there and ours are still loaded up. That's luck. Evidently de Brock didn't take up time relieving us. All right, let's hit leather."

None of the men needed telling twice. They leapt to their saddles, dug in their spurs, and rode like the devil, Jess bringing along Shorty's horse behind him so that its useful bedroll and other necessities would not be lost. From the saloon, as they travelled, there came only a few shots. The probable explanation was that de Brock and his men were too busy trying to stop the fire gaining a hold.

When they were a couple of miles from town, riding the trail which led directly to the mountains, Jess slowed the pace somewhat, Ox riding up beside him in the starlight.

"Seems we got outa that okay, Jess," he remarked. "An' if there's anythin' left of the Trail's End by mornin' I'll be surprised. Mebby we started a fire that'll burn all Yellow Gulch to th' ground afore it's through. That wouldn't be a bad idea, either. Make our job of wipin' out de Brock a whole lot easier."

Jess looked behind him into the violet sky with its brazenly winking stars.

"Yore too optimistic, Ox," he replied. "No sign of fire glow over there. De Brock and his boys musta got the blaze under control. Just as well they have 'cos I don't want the populace to be burned outa house an' home. It wouldn't help our cause a bit. At root we'd be considered responsible."

"Yeah, mebby yore right." Ox rubbed his head impatiently. "Dang me, there I go ag'in! Can't seem to figger things out. I thought it'd help: you say it wouldn't an' now I see yore right. Mebby I'm just plain dumb."

"Could be," Jess agreed, grinning. "But that doesn't mean yore not mighty useful, feller."

"Seems t'me, Jess, that we got precious little outa that saloon dust-up except the pleasure of pumping lead into some uv de Brock's boys. While it lasted it was the nicest thing I've done fur many a long month."

"We got more'n that," Jess rode on steadily. "For one thing we eliminated an unwanted sheriff, an' for another we found that most of the people are behind us but afraid to say so. I aim to start discoverin' next how many ranchers back us up. That'll be a solo job for me alone. There's also a mayor we've gotta take care of."

"Yeah! Sooner th' better fur as I'm concerned."

"From what I hear he's as much a mouthpiece for de Brock as the sheriff was. Those sort aren't wanted, an' when a man out here ain't wanted there's only one thing t' do with him."

"Yeah." Ox grinned widely in the starlight. "I guess yuh don't have ta tell me."

It was some time after midnight when at length Jess, Ox, and the boys were domiciled in the cave in the foothills which Jess himself had been using during the day-time. Having everything they needed for their immediate comfort they all had a meal, attended to the horses, and then sat in the starlight at the cave entrance, talking among themselves. They would have liked to smoke too but Jess forbade it, unless they concealed themselves in the cave. Even the glowing end of a cigarette would be visible for miles in the clear, sharp air of the Arizona night.

"Well, Jess, we've gotten this fur," Ox's voice remarked out of the gloom. "What happens next? Apart from yuh seein' how many ranchers is back uv us. I'm not one who likes loungin' around with nothin' t'deal with."

"As far as we're concerned nothing happens 'til de Brock starts something," Jess answered. "An we can't very well know if he starts something without working out a signal system with the ranchers. That's why I intend to take a ride around 'em tomorrow an' see if they're willin' to co-operate in bringing down de Brock."

"Mebby they'll be too leary t' give you any backing," Ox commented. "From what I've seen uv 'em around here de Brock's got th' livin' daylights scared outa them."

"Mebby. On the other hand, for their own good, they might be glad to be helpful. Then at some other time we're goin' to take care of the mayor. My aim is to eliminante everybody who supports de Brock and so gradually destroy his influence." "Yuh could leave the mayor t'me, Jess," Ox said, brooding. "I'd rub him out quicker'n a bug."

"I'll do it my own way, Ox, thanks."

"Lookee here, Jess, fast as you eliminate folks de Brock'll put somebody else in their places," one of the men objected. "That way we get no place."

"Don't be too sure of that," Jess told him. "Would you be willin' to take on the job of sheriff knowin' it would probably mean you'd die before long? Would you take on the job of mayor if you knew your predecessor had died 'cos he was a mayor? An' don't try an' give a snap answer: think it out first."

"I mightn't have no chance if a gun were fixed on me."

"Yes you would. The instinct of self-preservation is far stronger even than de Brock. I don't believe any man would take on an official job because of de Brock's say-so, not if it meant askin' for lead any time, anywheres. There are some things which even de Brock can't control, human nature f'r instance."

There was silence for a time, the men gazing out over the overlying waste of mist which blanketed the valley. In the direction of Yellow Gulch there was a faint amber glow from the kerosene lights in the main street, and that was all. The fire that had started had evidently been extinguished.

"D'yuh think de Brock's ever likely t'get this fur?" Ox asked at length.

"Mebby, but he'll have a hard job finding us. An' in any case with one or other of us always on th' lookout we'll see him first. One man alone up here can take care of an army, and I guess de Brock knows it. You'd best get some shut-eye, boys, includin' you, Ox," Jess said. "In 'bout two hours I'll wake some of you and hit the hay myself. So we'll work in shifts with somebody always on the alert."

"Okay." The big cowpuncher got lazily to his feet and vanished inside the cave.

The other men followed him, and presently all sound of movement ceased and Jess was left on his lonely vigil, his revolver at his side, his back against the rocks of the cave entrance. He smiled a little tautly to himself as he slowly began to realize what kind of a maelstrom he had precipitated. With nothing but a few hombres, he had launched himself into a win-or-die fight with one of the toughest cattlemen in the region.

He asked himself why he had done so. Where was the point in risking his neck to such an extent? And what did he get out of it when he finished? He decided that the answer lay in a slender girl with black hair and trusting, amber-coloured eyes. He could see her again now as he had seen her in the morning, the sunlight on her wealth of hair as she gave him the gun with which to protect himself.

"A girl doesn't give a strange man a gun unless she likes an' trusts him," Jess breathed, staring into the starlit distances where he knew the Calvert ranch to be. "Guess it'll be worth cleaning up this valley if only so's she can live in peace an' I can convince her old man that it pays to stand on your own two feet sometimes an' not go grovellin' on your knees to a tinhorn like de Brock."

Another thought also occurred to him as he sat pondering. He had promised to return the mare the girl had loaned him if he ever had the opportunity. Now that chance had arisen, even if tragically. He could use the horse which the unfortunate Shorty had had and return the mare, with thanks. It would be as good an excuse as any for visiting the Calvert spread again.

So, after breakfast the following morning, Jess was on his way, riding Shorty's mount and trailing the mare behind him. With Ox left as deputy in case of emergency, he had given orders for none of the men to move from the rendezvous until he returned, and to shoot any interlopers on sight. Ox had not seemed particularly taken with the idea, but by this time he had learned the necessity of obeying orders.

Indeed, with the thought of Fay Calvert on his mind, Jess was not particularly concerned with the machinations of de Brock for the time being. He believed, as any healthy man should, that business must be mixed with pleasure. None the less he was not so absorbed that he did not stay on the alert all the time he rode to the Calvert spread. Nobody interfered with him, however, and without his having seen a soul in the vast, sundrenched spaces he finally reached the forlorn-looking ranch towards ten o'clock.

It was the girl herself who opened the ranch-house door, and there was no mistaking the welcome which leapt into her eyes as she saw Jess standing outside.

"Mr Burton!" she ejaculated. "Back again so soon? This is better than I'd hoped for."

69

"Mornin', Miss Fay." Jess took off his hat and smiled at her. He knew that this time he was worth looking at. He was closely shaved and wearing a new shirt and kerchief, a very different man from the evil-smelling, dirt-caked figure who had sought shelter when escaping from the Square-8."

Abruptly the door opened wider, so suddenly that Fay, leaning on it, staggered back a little. Her father stood there, his gaunt face hard and friendless.

"Don't you think yore causin' enough trouble around here, Burton, without bringin' it right to our door?" he demanded. "Th' very fact that yore here leaves my gal an' me open to attack by de Brock's men if they're around."

"They're not," Jess told him quietly "An' even if they were I'm takin' the liberty of thinkin' you'd be man enough to fight it out against them."

Calvert glared. "I thought I'd made it clear to you that I don't intend to fight anybody, you or them. Now git off my spread, Burton, an' don't come back any more neither. I reckon I'm gettin' mighty tired of telling you."

Jess hesitated then he said, "I didn't come here just for the ride, Mr Calvert. I've brought back the mare your daughter loaned me. There she is, at the tie-rail. I've grabbed another horse, thanks to de Brock."

"Yuh nean you stole it?"

"I took it in return for my own. That's fair exchange, not stealin'."

"Have it your own way," Calvert said. "Now get goin'. An' I don't reckon it was so much honesty as led you to bring back th' mare. You thought you'd see my gal here

70

ag'in. Mebby figgered I'd be out. Yore wrong on both counts so you'd best be on the move."

"Before I go," Jess persisted, "you may as well know that I have other reasons too for being around here."

"I ain't interested!"

"Hear me out, Mr Calvert. I'm contacting the rest of the ranchers in this neighbourhood to see how many of 'em would be willin' to back me in a fight against de Brock. I have in mind a system of signals. You might like to hear more about a method for helpin' yourself."

"I danged well would not! If I leave de Brock alone I'm satisfied that he won't bother me neither."

"Dad, why do you keep on living in a fools' paradise?" the girl demanded angrily. "This passive attitude of yours won't get you anywhere if there is an attack. What sort of signalling have you in mind, Mr Burton?" she asked turning to Jess quickly.

"It's simple enough. All you have to do is build a heap of brushwood somewheres near here. Since it isn't the rainy season it should stay dry for several months. If yore attacked any time find some excuse to get out and light the stack. We'll see the smoke an' come an' help you out."

"An' where'll you be so's you can see the smoke?" Calvert snapped. "Haveta be somewheres pretty close, won't it?"

"We'll be in the — " Jess paused, studying the rancher's grim face then he shrugged. "In the mountains, Mr Calvert. We've a hide out there, an' I'm not sure that I'm not a durned fool for sayin' as much, not knowin' just where you stand. However, I'm bein' frank with you in the hope your attitude towards me will change in time."

"My attitude towards you won't ever change, Burton, so you can stop expectin' miracles. You know where I stand, neither for nor against. I shan't tell anybody where yore hidin', an' I shan't start buildin' beacon fires neither. De Brock won't bother me if I don't bother him. It's opposition that turns him sour, an' I don't aim to make any."

Jess grinned cynically. "You don't suppose he's taken all your cattle, bar these few you have left, without intendin' to finish the job, d'you? He'll take you for everythin' you've got before yore finished, includin' your daughter mebby. I can't see him passin' up the chance to make use of a girl as attractive as her; an' if only for her sake you should take steps to get protection."

"I reckon I can handle things in my own way, Burton, without your crazy notions."

As if to put an end to argument Calvert turned back into the ranch-house without adding further words. Jess looked after him, then to the girl again. She looked even more attractive this time than when he had first seen her. Her blouse and riding skirt had been abandoned for a simple cotton dress which gave her the true lines of a young woman.

"Well-er — " Jess looked awkward, his blue eyes upon her. "I-I guess that covers everythin', though I'd have bin a darned sight happier if I could have made your pop see reason. Still, there it is. All I can do now is be on my way and see the other ranchers around here."

"How will you know where to find them?" Fay asked simply. "They're pretty scattered."

"I know. But the territory isn't so huge. I'll find 'em all in due time."

"There are sixteen ranches around here over which de Brock is casting his shadow," the girl said. "Some are bunched together; others are widely separated. I know them all, and the best thing would be for me to act as your guide. I'm as interested as you are in seeing that you achieve success. If anything, more so."

Jess looked troubled. "That's mighty kind of you, Miss Calvert, but it'll be a dangerous job. I'm number one target for any gunman, remember, and if that gunman turns up he ain't likely to think twice 'bout puttin' lead between your shoulder-blades either. Should anythin' happen to you just because you stringed along with me I"d never forgive myself."

"I'll risk it. You have my mare waiting, so all I need do is change. Wait for me."

"An' how's about your pop?"

"I can deal with him." The girl smiled, and turned back into the ranch-house.

Evidently she could, for despite angry words which came from within the ranch, and then presently died away, Fay reappeared in a while in riding kit, a gun at her hip, and her mass of dark hair held back from her sunny face by a single childish blue ribbon.

Jess looked at her questioningly and she gave a shrug.

"Pa's not particularly pleased with my behaviour," she said, "but he knows he can't hold me when my mind's made up. I don't altogether like defying his wishes, but in this case his outlook is so utterly absurd."

Jess followed her down the steps and helped her into the mare's saddle. Then he vaulted to his own horse and side by side he and the girl rode through the drenching sunlight, presently coming to the rimrock which gave a vast, unhampered view of the territory immediately beyond the valley.

It had a breathtaking loveliness all its own. The very ground itself was pink and white with anemone blooms, outcroppings of yellow primrose and whispering bells peeping here and there. Further distant, upon the endless spaces of the distant mesa from which came the smell of the torrid desert, were the fields of golden brittle-bush and stately eight-foot high clusters of the Lord's Candles.

Even the looming mountain range nearby was in its finest garb, splashed with the silver-white of Apache plumes and the scarlet of the mallow. It was the season of the year when the rain gods of the Indians had been kind and Arizona had burst forth in its most voluptuous offerings. Here was a beauty in its wildest and sweetest sense, rioting in a world utterly alien to Wilton de Brock.

"I've lived around here since being twelve years of age and in ten years I've never tired of looking at this beauty in the spring," Fay said, as she and Jess rode along. "It's beautiful, too, by night, and in the winter when the rains and snows take their turn on the stage. But at this time of the year I know of nothing in the whole wide world to touch it!"

Jess glanced at her, smiling a little to himself.

"You must find it kinda lonely back there at the spread," he said. "I mean, yore young and you want life to keep you company. Yore too nice a girl to find it in a dump like Yellow Gulch. Far too good an education. An' livin' with your pop and his grouses must be as much as you can stand."

"It is a bit difficult sometimes," she admitted, sighing. "And dad's always so morose. The more he studies religion the more unhappy he seems to become. Not that there's anything wrong in religion," she added. "It's the way he interprets it. He's too literal in thinking one should forgive one's enemies. I'm not that way. I believe in fighting for what is right, no matter what the cost to myself. The pioneers of this land have always looked at things that way, so I suppose it's the common-sense view."

"In this part of the world, and with men like de Brock around, one has to," Jess said quietly. "He's the kind of man who is dying out from this country, ruthless, cold-blooded, intent on nothing but his own advancement no matter who is trampled down in the process. Somebody's got to stop him, an' somebody's going to! An' whilst I'm about it, Miss Calvert, I — "

"Please drop the prefix and the surname," she broke in, with a shy little smile. "I'd much rather have 'Fay'. It's so formal the other way and despite our rather … er … uneasy introduction we have become such firm friends."

Jess laughed. "I'm glad we have, Fay. That was what I was going to say, that I'm glad to find you trust me. It's a big thing which I've taken on, cleaning up the tyrannical gunplay in this territory, I was only thinking last night when I was perched on the watch in the mountains. You get to meditatin' on lots of things when everybody is asleep but yourself and there's nothin' but the loneliness of great spaces. Yeah, I guess I need all the friends I can get. An' don't forget to call me Jess."

The girl laughed, throwing back her head. Jess noticed how white and firm her teeth were. She breathed the atmosphere of the West. It was in the manner in which she handled her horse, the erectness of her figure, the tone of her voice, in her very attitude to life itself.

"That where we're headin'?" Jess asked presently, nodding to a distant ranch.

"Yes. That's the first of the sixteen — the Lucky-F. Mr Gorton and his wife and two young daughters live there, and all of them seem to have plenty of sense. They'll give you all the support you need, I'm sure."

Jess nodded and glanced about him as he rode. This was one of the most pleasurable journeys he had ever known: his only fear was that a gunman would suddenly appear and bring death or injury into the scene. But the landscape still remained deserted and he and the girl reached the Lucky-F without mishap some ten minutes later.

The moment they arrived at the gates of the yard, however, they could sense that there was something wrong. There was nobody in sight: the corrals and stables were empty; and in the centre of the yard itself was a monstrous circle of burned grass and debris where apparently a considerable amount of wooden material had been destroyed.

"I don't like this," Fay said, frowning as she dismounted. "It begins to look as though de Brock's been here already."

"Oh?" Jess glanced about him. "How can you tell?"

"His pet method is to burn up all the furniture and belongings when he drives out the ranchers. If they won't be driven out they get hanged. We wouldn't see this fire from our place: the height of the rimrock would hide it. The sooner we find out what has been happening the better."

Jess at her side, Fay headed for the ranch-house porch, to find the doors swinging wide and aimlessly in the strong, warm wind. Their guns at the ready they entered the shady hall, noting that it was bereft of furniture, and so entered the living room. Here they stopped, appalled for a moment by the shock they received.

The room had been completely stripped of furniture but in it were four people. A man and a woman, their hands secured behind them, swung from the central beam across the ceiling, ropes above their necks. Near to them, fastened back-to-back, and with one rope serving for both necks, were the two young daughters, aged perhaps eight and twelve. The bodies swung slightly in the wind through the smashed windows.

"It's ghastly!" Fay whispered, turning away for a moment but withal keeping a grip on herself. "It was right in my guess, it seems. De Brock's been here all right, or else his men have. Ranchers who won't quit are left like this as a warning to others to get out. And helpless children, too!"

"Yeah!" Jess' face was merciless. "Do your pop good to see this. Perhaps change his mind about bein' pleasant to the enemy. We'd best get outa here, Fay: there's nothing we can do."

Sobered by what they had seen they departed, riding to the next ranch some two miles distant. Here everything was in order, and thanks to Fay's help in backing him up Jess secured his much needed cooperation and a promise to light a beacon if an attack were made at any time.

By noon, when the sun was at its fiercest, they had made six calls and received full promise of cooperation in each case. At the Double Y they stayed for lunch and then rode quickly on again until by early evening every ranch had been visited. Of the fifteen ranchers interviewed twelve had agreed to the signal system: the others had hung back, clearly afraid to commit themselves to crossing de Brock, although there was little doubt they would come into line once they had seen somebody take the first plunge.

"I reckon twelve outa fifteens a high enough number to count on," Jess commented in satisfaction, as he and the girl ambled their horses back along the trail towards her own ranch. "An' many thanks for th' help you've bin. I certainly couldn't have gotten so much co-operation without you."

"Why shouldn't I help? I'm in this even more than you are. I know what you're driving at and it is as much in my interests as anybody's to see that you succeed. In fact there's only one thing lacking to my mind. I only wish I were a man and could ride beside you in every move you make against de Brock."

"I'm mighty glad yore not," Jess grinned.

"Wouldn't be half as nice to ride with you."

She smiled back at him and then demurely dropped the subject. Fifteen more minutes brought them back to her ranch and Jess lifted her down from the saddle.

"I don't know when I'll be back this way again," he said gently, his big hands holding her shoulders. "Just depends on how soon I get a free moment and how clear the trail is. But if I see a bonfire go up I'll be here pronto. Later, mebby, when all this trouble has been cleared up we may see quite a lot of each other."

"I'm counting on it," Fay said. "And it's going to seem an awful long time until it happens."

Jess hesitated, her slim, inviting form pressed close against him. One instinct prompted him to kiss her upturned face: another told him that he had not known her long enough. So he dropped his hands from her shoulders and turned to his horse, swinging into the saddle and then raising his hat.

"Bye, Fay," he smiled. "An' don't forget to tell your pop what we saw at the Lucky-F. It may change his mind. If it doesn't he should ride over and take a look-see for himself."

"I'll tell him," she promised. "Oh — there's something else, Jess — "

"Yeah?"

She motioned for him to stoop from the saddle so she could whisper in his ear — or so he expected. Instead he found his cheek brushed lightly with her lips.

"Just for luck, Jess," she murmured, and then she turned away quickly.

He grinned and straightened up again. "God help de Brock after that!" he thought, and with a dig of his spurs sent his horse ripping away across the grasslands. He looked back in the long, golden bars of the sunset until the girl had vanished in the distance.

5. Bushwacked

It was almost dark when Jess reached the mountain hide-out again. The men were squatting or lounging outside the cave entrance, the tethered horses some little distance away, their heads nodding sleepily. Ox, a cigarette clinging to his lower lip watched Jess through his eyelashes as he approached. There was a certain indefinable unfriendliness in his attitude.

"Enjoy yuhself with the girl friend?" he asked dryly "Or is that a needless question?"

Jess came to a halt, his gaze hard. "Meanin' what?"

"Just wonderin', that's all. From here we c'n see a bit uv the trail near th' rimrock. We saw you an' the gal headed that way this mornin'. Saw yuh comin' back too 'bout an hour ago. In th' meantime we've bin stuck here, waitin' fur anythin' that might happen, and in case yuh don't know it, Jess, it gets mighty monotonous."

"So?" Jess snapped.

"So it seems like yore gettin' most uv th' gravy!" Jess looked about him.

"Th' rest of you men feel that way?" he demanded.

None of the men answered. They either looked at each other or on the ground. Jess tightened his lips.

"For your information," he added, "the gal is Fay Calvert. Some of you may know her. She acted as my guide 'cos I didn't know where all the spreads were. And if I hadn't have had her with me I'd have bin several weeks gettin' myself initiated. What's more, I can't see what damned business it is of yours whether she rode with me or not."

"It's our business 'cos we can't afford t'have anybody else in on our plans," Ox retorted. "An' a woman least of all! I reckon that all the troubles that happen to a man are 'cos of a woman. As I figure it, she'll shoot off'n her face th' minnit it suits her. Then where'll we be?"

Jess hesitated for a moment, then suddenly he lashed out a right-hander with all his strength. Ox absorbed the blow and jolted back against the rocks, his cigarette dashed from his lips.

"That's just a reminder that I do as I like — within limits," Jess explained coldly. "An' if you've anything more t'say 'bout Fay Calvert keep it outa my hearing if yore wise. I don't aim to stand for it."

Ox heaved back into position, his eyes glinting. "Yuh don't suppose I'm takin' that frum you, do yuh?" he snapped. "I still say a woman's a danger if she knows too much. An' it bein' Fay Calvert makes it worse."

"What gave you that idea, y' big lug?" Jess demanded.

"I knows her well enough, an' her old man a durned sight better. He's loco on religion an' if the mood seized him he'd spit in our faces an' tell de Brock everythin' he knows 'bout us. I never did trust a guy who goes around smitin' a prayer book. Ain't nateral, t'my way uv thinkin'. Blasted cover-up fur sump'n else, most likely."

"I agree that old man Calvert's an awkward customer," Jess replied quietly, "but the girl isn't. She won't betray us. She's for us, one hundred per cent. I've ridden around with her long enough to be sure o' that."

"An' she knows where we are?" Ox asked.

"She knows we're in th' mountains, but that might mean just any place."

Ox spat contemptuously.

"Not to a gal who knows th' district like she does!" he retorted. "She knows that the only hideouts in this range are in these foothill caves. What's t'stop her sayin' as much? Not to de Brock, mebby, but to her old man."

"She isn't that sort," Jess answered, keeping tight rein on his temper. "Better realize that, Ox, an' save yourself a lot of grief."

"If that old has-been wanted t'know where we wus, yuh don't suppose he'd let a kid like his daughter keep her mouth shut, do yuh?"

"You're lookin' for trouble before it's here, Ox." Jess said. "Skip it. We'll start worryin' fast enough if anything happens. Don't forget that you never did have the gift of seein' ahead."

Ox said nothing. He lit up a fresh cigarette and scowled. Jess waited a moment and then went into the cave to rustle some food together for himself. Whilst he ate he explained in detail how he had spent the day and how many ranchers were willing to co-operate in the matter of signalling. There was no comment from amongst the men as he gave the facts.

"Which means that we'll have ta be constantly on our toes," he finished. "A smoke-signal by day; a fire-signal by night. Either, will mean that we're wanted pronto. You, Joe, had better take first look-out on that high rock yonder where you can see any smoke or fire there might be. You'll follow him, Jed, two hours later, then will come you, Ox. Then me. That duty has never t'be relaxed."

Ox and the rest of the men nodded assent and Joe, with first watch, went off to the rock in question and settled down on its blunt peak, a solitary figure against the glitering stars. Ox spat out his cigarette and slouched forward to where Jess was squatted in front of his meal.

"Sump'n I want to ask yuh, Jess ..."

"Okay, shoot, but take care what it is. If it's anythin' more to do with Fay Calvert I'm not in the mood to listen."

"Nope, nothin' t'do with her. I'm just wonderin' what about that mayor we wus goin' to take care of?"

"No hurry, is there?"

"Mebby not to your way uv thinkin', but I want some action!"

"Mebby you do, but to go lookin' for it is just stickin' your neck out!"

"It's my neck and I'm willing to risk it."

"Well, I'm not willin' that you should," Jess retorted. "If anything happens to you it can happen to all of us. Quit thinkin' of yourself for once and give the rest of us a chance."

Ox rubbed the back of his neck uncertainly. "Well-okay," he agreed grudgingly. "But I still say that if de Brock doesn't start somethin' fur sometime we'll just sit here on our backsides an' do nothin', which ain't my idea of fun. I say, let us begin trouble, startin' with th' mayor."

"What you say doesn't matter," Jess told him. "Yore not the boss of this outfit, Ox."

"Mebby we"d get on better if I wus! At least I wouldn"t be aimin' to mix wimmin in my plans!"

"Why, you big, overgrown gorilla, I'll — " Jess leapt to his feet, his fist retracted to deal the massive cowpuncher a haymaker, then he stopped and glanced round as Joe came suddenly into the cave.

"A fire!" he gasped. "Be 'bout six miles away. Must be somethin' doin', Jess."

"Let's go," Jess said brusquely. "I can tell which ranch it is as we ride. You, Joe, stay behind and keep guard over everything. The rest of you come with me."

The abrupt call to action killed all private squabbling for the moment. In five minutes each man, except Joe, was riding at full speed down the mountain trail, watching the small and wavering red spot in the distance which beckoned them.

"Looks like the Double-Y where Miss Calvert and I had lunch today," Jess said presently. "An' that's a tidy ride! Let's speed things up a bit."

He goaded his horse to the limit, and not to be outdone the men with him did likewise. In a thunder of hoofs they swept across the pasture-lands which rolled away from the foothills, presently hitting the roughly defined trail which led out to the mesa. From here they had the distant visions of the beacon fire clearly before them.

And now they beheld something else. Not only the beacon was burning but towering piles of wood as well. Dim figures were visibly going back and forth to the ranch-house, carrying material out and dumping it in the blaze.

"Same old technique!" Jess commented grimly. "Burnin' up th' furniture, an' unless old man Glenthorpe an' his wife have gotten away they'll be strung up. Take it easy from here on," he added. "Anythin' can happen.

One mistake on our part and this is th' last fire-raisin' party we'll attend." A hundred yards from the blaze he jumped down from the saddle and drew his guns. Detailing one of the men to watch the horses, he, Ox, and the others went swiftly forward, not towards the fire but round the back of the ranch-house.

"What's th' big idea?" Ox demanded. "We came here t'blast hell outa these jiggers, didn't we? Not creeep round corners. You lost yore nerve, Jess?"

"Use your head!" Jess told him. "We don't want that fire glare showin' where we are, do we? Besides, it's probable that Glenthorpe an' his wife have bin hung in the livin' room: we've them to free first of all."

"Yeah!" Ox agreed blankly. "Dang me, I never thought uv that!"

"You wouldn't. Come on!"

They entered the ranch-house through the open back door and, uninterrupted at this point, went quickly through to the living room. An old lamp was burning on the table and as yet the old rancher and his wife were still alive. They lay on the floor, tightly bound, but otherwise apparently unhurt, struggling on savagely to release themselves.

"Thank God that yuh came, Jess!" Glenthorpe panted, relief on his weather-beaten face. "I risked lightin' th' beacon. These hoodlums don't know why I did it; they said it wus nice o' me to prepare a fire for burnin' up my possessions. They've 'bout taken everything," he added bitterly. "Furniture, private papers, beddin' — all the lot."

"Okay, okay, take it easy," Jess murmured. "Jed, untie 'em. Th' rest of you get ready."

He had hardly finished his sentence before two of the gunmen came back and headed for the table, one of the last articles of furniture remaining in the room. They had just about reached it when they realized that things were not as they had left them.

"What the — " One of the men stopped and stared at Jed as he busily untied the rancher. "Where in blue tarnation did you come from?"

"Hold it!" Jess ordered, stepping out of the shadows. "Drop that gun! You too!" he barked to the second man. "Ox, take their weapons."

Ox did so, grinning at the thought of what was to come.

"Get out on the porch and call your pals here," Jess instructed. "I'll be right behind you. One wrong word an' yore finished. Go ahead!"

Unable to do anything else the sullen gunmen did as ordered. It brought the four remaining men from the blazing bonfire of furniture. Only when they got into the dim living room to behold guns relentlessly fixed on them did they realize what had happened.

Jess considered them, thinking, as Glenthorpe and his wife got slowly on their feet.

"Unfortunately," Jess said, "I can't make you return the furniture you've destroyed, but I can an' will extract payment for it." He looked across at the rancher. "What do y' reckon was the value of the stuff burned, Mr Glenthorpe?"

"'Bout five hundred dollars" worth, I'd say. The private papers had no value, 'cept personal. Nothin' we can do 'bout them, I guess."

"We can take it in kind," Jess decided. "How many papers were taken?"

"Five. Private deeds an' such."

"Okay." Jess meditated for a moment or two and then nodded to himself. "Right! Five lashes for the papers taken. That's five lashes for each of these hoodlums."

"Yuh think yuh can do that?" one of the men roared. "We'll durned well show yuh whether — "

"Yeah, we can do it all right," Ox interrupted, his jaw jutting. "I took many a heatin' back at the Square-8 so it'll be a real pleasure t'hand some uv it back." He put down his gun and very deliberately rolled his sleeves back along his heavily muscled arms.

"Gunmen like these are usually well supplied with greenbacks," Jess added. "Frisk 'em, Ox, and see if y' can find five hundred. If there happens t'be more we'll take it just th' same."

Ox grinned, seized the nearest man by the shirt collar, and then went through his pockets by the simple expedience of ripping away each one. With each man he did the same, administering a killing blow in the face wherever he met resistance. The sum total of the money he collected was four hundred and eighty dollars. He held the money up in the air in his massive hands.

"Okay, that's near enough," Jess said. "Now we want a whip. Get one, Mr Glenthorpe. A stockwhip for preference: one that'll sting like hell."

"There's a whip in one of the stables," the rancher replied. "But do you think   you —"

"Yeah, I do!" Jess snapped. "Havin' it taken outa their hides every time they strike will make these owl-hooters think twice. Hop to it, Ox."

"You betcha, Jess."

Ox hurried from the living room through the open window. In a few minutes he returned, the stockwhip in his powerful hand. Obviously enjoying himself, he tied the first man across the table, ripped off his shirt, and then swung the lash with all the power of his iron muscles.

At the end of delivering the punishment upon each man he was winded and sweating but grinning sadistically. Jess nodded as the groaning gunmen staggered by the wall, trying to struggle back into their shirts. Finally they gave it up, their flayed backs too tender to bear the friction of the cloth. Jess studied them silently, no hint of compassion in his coldly glinting eyes.

"That will teach you, my friends, that to go around pillaging and murdering doesn't pay," he said presently. "It's a small punishment for the things you've done. I'd have killed you all only I don't know which of you are really responsible for murder: so this will have to suffice for the present. I'm referring to the hangin' of Gorton an' his wife an' two daughters at the Lucky-F. What they went through at your filthy hands Gods knows, an' I'm only too sorry I'm forced by a sense of justice to leave you in one piece, so's you can recover an' I suppose be as vile again. But I'm warnin' you, if yore caught molesting any of the ranchers again you'll hang on the spot! Okay, boys, put 'em on their horses and tie their hands to the saddle backs."

Knowing he could safely leave Ox to finish the job, Jess relaxed as the whipped men were bundled out of the room. He patted Glenthorpe on the shoulder.

"That finishes tonight's work, Mr Glenthorpe," he said. "An' this money should help you out. Here's a few hundreds of mine too which originally belonged to de Brock. I reckon it oughta set you on your feet again. The signal system remains in case anythin' more happens, though I don't think it will for a long time. Those hoodlums have had the biggest beatin' of their lives and they know what they'll get if they try ag'in."

"We can never be grateful enough to yuh, Jess," the rancher whispered, and his wife nodded urgent confirmation.

"That's okay," Jess smiled. "It was about time somebody hit back around here anyway. Think nothin' of it."

*

Wilton de Brock, however, thought a good deal when towards the early hours of the morning his bruised and bloodstained minions tottered into his living room in the Square-8 ranch-house. He said nothing for a moment, so astounded was he; then gradually rage began to darken his colour.

He got slowly to his feet, the deadly gleam in his eyes betraying his fury.

"And what the devil happened to you?" he demanded. "What the devil happened?"

"Burton uv course!" the leader of the men snarled, too hurt to be civil.

"Burton, eh?" de Brock's eyes narrowed. "What did he do?"

"He breezed in out of nowheres with some uv his boys an' that tough gorilla Ox set about us with a stockwhip. They took all our money an' then Ox set us off on our cayuses like this, our hands tied. We got 'em free after a while. Next time Burton sez he'll hang us on the spot. That's what he calls bein' lenient."

"And you mean that you failed to get rid of Glenthorpe and his wife?"

"Course we failed! They're sittin' as pretty as they ever wus. Burton took care uv that."

The gunmen waited, breathing hard and wincing as de Brock paced slowly up and down, tireless despite the lateness of the hour. His mouth was set in a thin, hard line. Presently he seemed to make up his mind.

"Burton couldn't just have dropped out of the sky," he said finally. "Some kind of signal must have attracted him."

"Yeah — a beacon," one of the men said. "We didn't git the idea at first, but we have since."

"In other words, if you'd have used your brains, granting you have any, the whole debacle could have been sidestepped? At least you have confirmed my inner opinion that all of you are as senseless as animals. A beacon, eh?" de Brock mused. "Flames by night and smoke by day, like the Indians. Not very original, perhaps, but most effective."

He came to a halt, fingering his chin. He spoke again abruptly:

"Very well, this must be taken care of. Tomorrow, in daylight, I'll take personal charge of a raid. We'll reinforce our numbers with every man we can. I'll even bring in the mayor to ride with us. The more the better. We'll ride to the Crooked-K, which has been standing in my way for longer than I like. And we'll see that the beacon is lighted. Then when Jess Burton and his men come riding in we'll ambush 'em and give them the lesson of their lives. Certainly that low-down cowpoke isn't going to upset my plans in this fashion. Now get out, the lot of you, and clean up. You're making my home filthy, and besides, you have got to be ready for morning."

"I've the feelin', boss, that I'll not be able t'do anythin' tough for weeks," one of the men groaned.

"Then get rid of that feeling," de Brock suggested curtly. "I've no room for lily-whites in my outfit. If you feel unable to join us," he grinned sardonically, "you may prefer a long rest from which you'll never be disturbed."

*

At breakfast in the hide-out the following morning Jess and his boys were in a happy mood.

They had had plenty of action; they had beaten the pants off de Brock's gunmen, and not one of them had been hurt. In fact, in retrospect, the adventure of the night seemed as if it had been too good to be true.

"If it's all goin' t'be as simple as that it's not goin' t'be much fun," Ox complained, helping himself to beans. "Just thrashin' them hombres last night an' takin' their money wus too Sunday-school fur me. I'd sooner have stretched their blasted necks, which wus what they deserved. I still say yuh was too kind to 'em, Jess. Pity I wasn't in charge uv that lot."

Jess grinned. "Nice, gentle guy, ain't you? Be satisfied for th' moment, with what's happened, Ox, an don't think we've a bed of roses ahead of us, either! You don't suppose de Brock'll sit down to what we did, do you?"

"I guess not. I'm expectin' him t'come gunnin' fur us at any moment, an' I kinda wish he would. I'd like nothin' better'n to flatten him."

"He has more sense than you think, Ox," Jess answered, shaking his head. "Comin' up here is the last thing he'd risk. If he can he'll try an' trap us. Tonight I figger he might try another raid, just for the sake of drawin' us into it. If he does we'll be ready for him. Won't be the first time we've anticipated an ambush an' given our enemies a thrashin'."

"It's a long ways to tonight," Ox sighed, chewing as he contemplated the sunny morning landscape.

"I like action all th' time else I get sorta quarrelsome. Which reminds me, Jess, I said things last night I didn't mean. I was gettin' edgy, I reckon. Y' know by now the kind uv guy I am. Sez what I thinks an' can't plan t'save me life."

"Okay, it's forgotten," Jess responded, shrugging. "Unless y'feel like rakin' it up again when I tell you I'm goin' this mornin' to see Miss Calvert."

"What fur?" Ox's eyes narrowed in sudden suspicion and the men around him paused in their eating for a moment to hear what was coming next.

Jess got to his feet and looked round on the assembly.

"To pay my respects, for one thing, an' to warn old man Calvert that he'll have t'be on the watch against attack from now on. If de Brock finds out I'm pretty thick with Fay Calvert he'll give her ranch special attention, perhaps try an' strike at me through her. I'm expectin' it, an' for that reason Calvert's got t'be convinced of his danger an' converted to a beacon warnin' if at all possible."

Ox shrugged, but if he disliked the idea of a further visit to Fay he did not say so.

"I'll keep watch whilst yuh go," he volunteered, "but for Pete's sake, Jess, don't stay away 'til evenin'."

"I aim to stay away as long as I see fit."

"Yeah, I know, but it'll have me on the jumps wonderin' how much that gal's learnin' from yuh."

"She won't learn any more than I choose to tell her," Jess said simply, putting on his hat. "Suppose you let me worry about that, huh? Be seein' you later?"

He turned and left the cave, heading for his tethered horse a few yards down the narrow trail. He kept on the alert all the time he rode through the foothills but he gained the Calvert spread without any trouble.

Apparently Fay had seen him coming for she opened the door as he was mounting the steps of the porch.

"Jess!" She took his big hand as he extended it towards her, and smiled a greeting. "I wondered how long it would be before you came again?"

"And your father?" Jess enquired. "That's what I came about, partly, to know what reaction he showed when y' told him what we discovered at the Lucky-F yesterday?

"No reaction at all," she responded, sighing.

"What! You mean that even that kind of butchery doesn't stir him?"

"Apparently not. Anyways, his views have not changed in the slightest. He's out at the moment," Fay added. "Gone into town for provisions."

"An' leave you here to take whatever may come? That it? It sure wouldn't do if you were my daughter. You'd ride with me, where I'd know you were safe."

"I can look after myself," she responded. "Dad and I don't hit it off so well together these days, remember. He knows I think he's cowardly for not standing up to de Brock, and it's sort of strained our relationship."

"Yeah," Jess murmured. "A pity, of course, but I guess that's the way things are. Not that I'm taking the blame for it, even though he'd like me to."

"You've nothing to blame yourself for, Jess. You've done all you can." Fay suddenly changed the subject. "I believe you were busy giving de Brock a welcome at the Double-Y last night? I heard all about it this morning. Mr Glenthorpe's telling every rancher within reach what happened, how you saved him and his wife and thrashed those gunmen."

"Yeah, de Brock's men certainly got more'n they expected," Jess grinned. "Just as they will next time 'til finally they lose their appetite for murder and pillage. Once that happens de Brock's power'll be broken." He thought for a moment and then continued, "I guess I had another reason too for coming here. I thought that what happened last night when we saved Glenthorpe might have given your old man the notion that it mightn't be such a bad idea after all t'have a beacon ready."

"I asked him about that only this morning, when Mr Glenthorpe brought the news, but dad won't hear of it. No use trying, Jess. You'd waste your time."

"Too bad," he muttered. "Going to make it tough for you as well as me. I'll never have an easy moment with no means of knowin' if yore being attacked or not."

The girl smiled. "If we're attacked you'll see a signal all right," she promised. "I'll set fire to that manzanita thicket over yonder" — she nodded to it — "and it being dry it'll be every bit as good as a beacon. There's no need to build wood up in readiness whilst that's there."

Jess glanced at it and nodded. "Good enough." He fidgeted with his hat in his hands and smiled awkwardly. "Which seems to about cover everythin', Fay, more's the pity."

"What do you intend to do now?" she enquired. "Go back to your mountain retreat?"

"Oh, just be a matter of killin' time 'til somethin' happens, an' I don't expect that to be before night." Fay contemplated the sunny glory of the morning for a moment; then she asked:

"Think we might go for a ride together? Plenty I'd like to talk about, Jess. We've a lot in common."

"So I noticed yesterday when you kissed me goodbye. I haven't forgotten the feel of that!"

Fay gave her shy smile and looked away.

"I'll change," she said, and returned to the ranch-house.

And at the moment she did so, Ox, back at the mountain retreat, looked up suddenly from his half dozing attitude inside the cave as Jed, on look-out, came bounding in.

"A smoke signal!" he said breathlessly. "Ways across th' valley! Can't exactly see where it's a-comin' frum, otherwise I'd know if it were genooine. Mebby a nateral fire, but mebby it also means trouble."

"Whichever it is we've gotta find out," Ox responded, surging to his feet. "Jess would haveta be away! I told him wimmin ain't no use in this racket! When yuh want him he ain't t'be found! Okay, I'll do th' job myself. Git on your hosses, boys, 'cept you, Jed. Stay here on guard."

Within a few minutes they were on their way. It was as they came within full sight of the pasture lands from where the smoke was issuing that they could see it belonged to the Crooked-K ranch; and to judge from the noise of gunshots and vision of milling men on horseback, a good deal was going on.

Ox, his right-hand gun ready, surveyed the scene as he rode. Then he glanced at the men with him.

"I ain't one fur fancy business an' goin' through back doors, like Jess," he said. "We'll ride straight into it an' shoot th' jiggers down. Let's go."

He dug his spurs deeply into his horse's flanks, hurtling across the remaining stretch of grassland separating him from the Crooked-K. He did not even have the chance to fire his gun, however. A rifle exploded from nowhere and he went crashing down into darkness with an intolerable pain searing his arm.

When the mists cleared again he was lying on his back on a wooden floor, his wrists and feet secured, dried blood clotting his arm. He moved it stiffly, winced and then gazed about him. In a row, securely trussed, were the men with whom he had been riding. Nearby, his chair on its hind legs, sat a guardian cowpoke, rifle across his knees, a wisp of straw working up and down in his ceaselessly moving jaws.

"Some guy plugged me!" Ox breathed, scowling.

"I did," the guard told him. "Good shot, huh? Only sorry I couldn't finish yuh but th' boss said not t' scramble any of yuh up too much. He's got his own plans."

"If I've a bullet lodgin' in me arm it's only common humanity that I should have a sawbones fix me up," Ox said bitterly. "Or mebby yuh don't know what common humanity is?"

"What's the use when yore goin' t'die anyway?" The guard grinned. "An' yuh ain't got no bullet in yuh. It scored yuh hide, that's all. A tough guy like you ought't even ter feel it. If yuh do, then it's just too bad!"

Ox tightened his lips and said no more. He had gathered by now that he was seated in the empty living room of the Crooked-K. Of the normal occupants there was no sign.

"Looks like we'd ha' done better after all t'get in the back way," growled the man seated next to Ox. "We ran us smack into an ambuscade and got ourselves hogtied afore we could turn around. We've bungled this properly, Ox. Th' guy who owned this spread, an' his wife, have bin hanged in th' stable. We saw it happen. Right now the furniture's burnin' up outside. An' I guess it won't be long afore plenty happens to us too."

"Jess wouldn't ha' messed it up like this," growled the man at the end of the row. "I reckon he had th' right idea creepin' in the back way. That's yur trouble, Ox, no sense uv plannin'!"

"Aw, quit beefin'!" Ox spat back at him. "I did me best, didn't I? Anyways, I came here, which is more'n Jess has done, spendin' his time neckin' with that Calvert gal when he oughta be attendin' to business!"

"So that's where Burton is, huh?" the guard asked. "Th' boss wus quite disappointed not ter find him here."

He broke off and turned as the living room door opened and de Brock himself came in. He advanced until

97

he was within a few feet of the bound men; then he stood surveying them.

"Not quite as cocksure this time, my friends, eh?" he asked dryly. "Only pity is that I have you scum and not Burton, the man I really want. Where is he?"

"Out with Fay Calvert, boss, neckin' some place," the guard replied.

"Oh!" de Brock raised his eyebrows. "And leaving you men to take the responsibility, eh? Not very good leadership on his part, is it?"

"You shut up!" Ox retorted, struggling fiercely with his ropes. "What Jess does is no business of yours, or mine either, even if I did open me mouth too wide. An' I'll get you, too, yuh ornery skunk, for blabbin' about it!" He added, glaring at the guard. "Yuh've got the finger on me right now, I admit, but it won't always be so. God help yuh when I get my hands on yuh filthy neck!"

"The Calvert girl, eh?" de Brock mused for a while. "Mmm, I quite admire Burton's choice. Fine girl! Quite surprising, too, considering her psalm-smitin' hypocrite of a father." He looked at Ox and smiled coldly. Thank you for the information, Ox. I'll see that Burton is picked up, and the girl too if need be. First, though, I have you and your friends to deal with. I could shoot you, of course, but that would soon be over, and I am bearing in mind that you have given me a tremendous amount of trouble. I also recall that you gave several of my men a most uncomfortable time at the business end of a stockwhip. Oh, Mr Mayor, what do you think should be done with these cutthroats?"

De Brock turned as the tubby, baby-faced Mayor Anderson came into the room, followed by several of the gunmen who had completed their furniture-burning activities.

"Done with them?" Anderson looked uneasily at the cold, murderous stares of the bound men. He was safe enough at the moment, but if to please de Brock he opened his mouth too wide, and if there was any slip-up later, his life wouldn"t be worth a plug nickel.

"The mayor, huh?" Ox breathed venomously, glaring at him. "I always knew yuh wus on de Brock's side, Mayor. So does Jess; but I never figgered yuh'd ride with one uv these necktie parties."

"I ... er ... am Mr de Brock's servant," the mayor explained nervously.

"Course yuh are, yuh fat-bellied traitor," Ox sneered. "There ain't hardly a guy in this blasted territory that ain't!"

"Speak up, Mr Mayor," de Brock invited, smiling amiably. "With absolute certainty of security you can say what shall be done with these hoodlums. They murdered the sheriff, don't forget, or at least Burton did, but these men were party to it. They also shot that rancher in the Trail's End. Above all, they are upsetting our plans for justifiable expansion. So, what shall it be?"

"Per-perhaps shooting would be quickest, an' safest," the mayor suggested, with a sidelong look at Ox's ugly, menacing face. "There isn't any real cause for a great deal of ceremony, is there?"

"And leave bullets around for any possible Governor to trace if the bodies should ever be found, and if a Governor ever gets this far?" de Brock shook his head.

"Oh, no, Mr Mayor! We have been so careful to avoid the use of bullets, hence the hangings. But we need something even more lasting than that, this time. Something total!"

The mayor said nothing. He was perspiring with uncertainty, licking his lips.

"I had thought of the bonfire outside here," de Brock finished, contemplating it through the window. "Yes, that would do excellently. I shall leave it entirely in your care, Mr Mayor, much though I would have liked to stay and watch the fun."

"My care!" the fat mayor ejaculated, starting. "But-but I thought it was you who always gave the orders around here, Mr de Brock?"

"Indeed I do, and am doing. It will be your task to carry them out to the letter. You see, I have Burton to think of, and the sooner I get to the Calvert ranch and welcome him home again with Miss Calvert the better I'll like it."

"Mind the step!" Ox suggested, as de Brock turned away.

The cattle baron hesitated, half raised his fist, and then dropped it again. Time was too pressing for him to delay.

6. Retribution

To Jess, lounging in the long grass about a mile from the Calvert ranch with Fay beside him, trouble and gunplay might have been at the other end of the earth. At first he and the girl had set out to take a rambling ride together, but two considerations had made them change their minds.

The heat of the sun was overpowering for one thing; and for another they would have made themselves targets. So now they lay side by side, contemplating drifting cumuli far overhead in the cobalt-blue sky, their horses nodding sleepily nearby.

"If all life were as pleasant as this I reckon I'd be satisfied," Jess grinned, stretching out his long legs and putting his hands behind his head.

"No you wouldn't."

"Huh?" Jess looked at the girl. Her face was close to his, her amber-coloured eyes mischievous. The mass of dark hair had half blown over her face in the gentle wind. "You wouldn't," she repeated. "You're a man of action, Jess, not an idler. Lying in the grass looking at me would very soon get tedious."

His grin broadened. "I can think of lots of unpleasanter ways of spendin' a spring morning. For instance, fancy lyin' lookin' at de Brock."

The girl looked up into the sky again, her features slowly becoming thoughtful.

"Jess, supposing you do wipe out de Brock — "

"Supposin'! There's no supposin' about it, Fay. One of us is goin' to die with his boots on before this little joyride is over, an' it ain't goin' to be me. I made up my mind on that long ago."

"All right then, when you have cleaned up de Brock, what do you propose to do? Run the valley yourself?"

"It doesn't need runnin', Fay. It would run itself if the settlers in it are given a chance to rear their cattle an' walk around with their wives an' kids in the sunlight an' starlight without the fear of a rope around their necks, or that their cattle disappear. That is all I'm aimin' for, peace in Yellow Gulch. If I do anythin' official at all it'll be to get myself sworn in as sheriff, not by a phoney mayor like we've got now, but one appointed by the nearest State Governor. Then later mebby Yellow Gulch an' the State it's in will be incorporated into a big Federal Union. It's comin', y'know, when all the States'll be united under one legislation."

"In a valley as quiet as you'll want it, Jess, your job as sheriff would be a mighty easy one. You'd get bored, and once that happened you'd be unbearable with an impetuous nature like yours."

"Oh, I dunno. I'd have other interests, too," Jess sat up and squinted into the blazing sunlight. "A ranch, cattle, good markets, things expandin' … " He paused and then grinned with the awkwardness which showed he was embarrassed. "An' a decent woman t'look after the home side," he added. "I reckon that's an essential thing. Or mebby I'm talking outa turn?"

"You've done nothing else but talk out of turn ever since you laid eyes on my gal!"

Jess looked behind him in surprise; as he did so the lash of a whip struck him savagely across the face. It whirled again, but this time he ducked and jumped up. Old man Calvert came down the bank quickly, caught Fay by one arm and dragged her to her feet. Holding her tightly he glared at Jess, the riding-whip in his free hand.

"I thought I told yuh to keep away frum my gal!" he panted in fury. "The moment I turn my back I find her gone. I start a-looking for her an' after trampin' round the countryside fur God knows how long I see the hosses. Then you an' her stuck here in th' grass."

"We were just talkin', that's all." Jess kept his voice under control, a red weal rising across his cheek.

"Sure that was all?" Calvert sneered. "I reckon a hombre like you mightn't be content with just talkin'!"

Jess' mouth set hard but he did not say anything. Not that he had any particular respect for old man Calvert, but he had a great deal for Fay.

Fay tore herself free of her father's clutch. "Dad, how can you say such things?" she cried angrily. "There is nothing wrong with Jess an' me sitting in the shade here talking and if you think there is — "

"I think what I please, gal!" her father told her, with a stony glance. "I've asked y' to behave like a decent woman, an' live with me, your father, in a right an' proper way. It's your duty t'me with your mother gone, rest her soul. Instead you go around with this gunman! This hombre! It don't take much imagination t' guess what he — "

"Take it easy, Mr Calvert," Jess warned. "The last thing I want to do is hit you. Yore a much older man than me for one thing, an' yore Fay's father for another.

If those two factors weren't in th' way I might do plenty. Don't go too far, that's all. I guess you gotten your thinkin' all tangled up. Fay an I have a likin' for each other, sure, an' that's the top an' bottom of it. The sooner you realize a man an' woman get that way sometimes, like you and your wife must have done once, I guess, the better for everybody."

Calvert ignored him. He turned to his daughter in a fury.

"D'you mean, gal, you've sold your soul to this tramp?" he asked, staring at her fixedly.

"You don't have to be Biblical about it, dad," she replied with some spirit. You make the mistake of basing everybody's actions on those of Scriptural characters and — "

"All right!" Calvert interrupted, raising a hand. "All right! I've nothin' more t'say. You've chosen this man instead of doin' your duty to me, so you can stay with him! He'll only drag yuh down into sin an' perdition, an' when that happens I don't want it t'be said that yore any flesh an' blood of mine! Don't come back home again ever!"

Calvert turned and stalked away over the grass bank, leaving Fay staring after him, tears suddenly brimming in her eyes.

"Dad! Dad, for heaven's sake — "

She half moved to follow him, hesitated, then turned back to where Jess stood in silence. She looked at him dumbly and shrugged her slender shoulders.

"Jess, what do I do?" she asked helplessly. "I've done nothing wrong. Neither of us have. He behaves so — so crazily." Her voice broke as she tried to control her

104

emotions. "I've never told you quite how crazily. This is only one sample of it. I'm sure Mother dying did something to him. He's got the idea that I should take her place, never have any fun, never look at any man, behave like I was old and withered. Just look after him — him — him." She caught up her last words in a shivering little gasp and then stood biting her lower lip.

Jess moved over to her and put an arm about her shoulders. He hugged her gently to him. "If he wants it that way, Fay, leave him be," he advised, with a shrug. "I'm well able to take care of you, even though I don't know what the boys back at the hideout will say. Later, when all this business is cleared up 'til either become sheriff and get regular money that way or else I'll work in some rancherls outfit."

There was silence for a moment, Fay doing her best to smile through her tears. Then Jess spoke again.

"Say, look, I'm forgettin'. You can't just walk out. You've no spare clothes or anythin', have you?"

"Nothing but what I'm wearing," she answered miserably. "I suppose I could buy some more in the town, only I haven't any money with me."

"Then we'll go back to your spread and get whatever belongs to you. Yore entitled to that — "

Jess stopped suddenly, his grip tightening on the girl's shoulder. In surprise she glanced at him and saw him staring as rigidly as an image into the distance. She gave a start at the vision of a towering column of black smoke belching into the hot morning sky from beyond a distant rimrock of mountain.

"Something wrong!" he said abruptly, releasing her. "A ranch afire. Either accidental or else de Brock's pulled a fast one, which is the very thing I've bin expecting would happen. In any case I've got t'look."

He stood hesitating, divided in his allegiance.

The girl made up his mind for him.

"I'll come with you," she said, hurrying towards her horse. "Only I've no gun."

Jess handed her one of his own. "You have now," he told her, lifting her to the saddle. "One will do for me. I don't like doing a job like this with you in th' thick of it, but mebby it's safer than leavin' you stranded."

He said no more, dug in his spurs, and darted his mount forward. The girl kept up with him, and at a spanking pace they hit the ill-defined trail which led out to the mesa. Within ten minutes they had come within sight of the fire itself.

"It's the Crooked-K!" the girl exclaimed. "And that's not just a beacon fire, either! Look at the size of it! Probably it's burning furniture."

"De Brock!" Jess muttered. His eyes narrowed. "An' for some reason he's struck in daylight. For some good reason, mebby." He was silent for a moment or two gazing intently into the distance. "I don't see any sign of Ox or th' boys but I'll gamble they've ridden in to see what it's all about. Best go carefully, Fay; anythin' can happen."

"I can see men moving about near the fire," she said, straining her eyes.

"Yeah. Quite a lot of 'em. Don't know whether they're friends or enemies, an' we daren't go near enough to make sure. Here, quick! In this hollow!" he broke of sharply. "A lone rider's coming!"

He wheeled his horse round, the girl doing likewise. Only just in time they ducked out of sight behind the high ridge of a grass bank, and dismounted. Watching intently they saw the rider pass at a considerable distance, flogging his horse at a furious pace.

"It's de Brock," Jess muttered. "An' too far away for me to take one shot at him, worse luck. Somethin' queer goin' on," he added, reflecting for a moment or two. "de Brock isn't hurt an' nobody's followin' him, which seems to show he's gotten the upper hand. Looks t'me like that big lunkhead Ox has gummed himself up somehow. He's one of those kind of mugs who can never plan things out properly. Bet he's cursin' me too for not bein' around when the signal went up."

"Well, we did see it finally," the girl replied, "so we've nothing to blame ourselves for."

"This," Jess muttered, "takes thinking about. We've got to ride straight into the danger and still win somehow. Must be a way."

"One thing we could do," the girl said, after a while. "I could ride up to the ranch in the ordinary way and so take their attention."

"Dangerous!" Jess decided, pondering.

"No doubt of that, but I'm pretty sure they wouldn't shoot me, not without express orders from de Brock himself, and we know he won't be there. Whilst I'm holding their attention you could creep in round the back way or something."

"Far too big a risk for my likin'," Jess said, gazing at the girl. "If anything should happen to you — "

"It's my risk, not yours, and I'm prepared to take it."

"Mebby, but for all we know de Brock has probably given orders to shoot any strangers on sight. An' that'll include you."

"I don't think so," Fay answered, shaking her head. "He's careful whom he shoots: that's why there are so many hangings. My guess is that he doesn't want to leave tell-tale bullets lying all around. Anyway, Jess, my mind's made up," she decided, and gettng to her feet she moved to her horse. Before Jess could stop her she had swung into the saddle and spurred the beast out of the depression and up to the pastureland.

"Durned crazy," he breathed, "but the gal's got nerve, an' that's what I like."

He mounted his own horse and watched the girl's distant, retreating figure in the sunlight. Whatever might happen now he could not alter it, so he began to put his own plan into action. He rode hard, circuiting the ranch in a detour which kept him a mile away from it, cutting through every low-lying fold of ground he could find, until he had come to a point where he was at the rear of the spread. Only then did he start to hurtle his mount towards it, his approach concealed by the bulk of the ranch-house building and stables.

He rode his horse straight toward the fence surrounding the rear of the yard, dismounted, and then went across the yard with his gun at the ready. As he had hoped, all attention was concentrated at the front of the building, where the furniture bonfire was still burning.

Moving in swift silence he crept round the side of the ranch-house until he had reached a point where, from an angle, he could see the front of the spread. Amidst the smoke-wreaths, which obscured the view at times, he could descry Ox and his men, firmly bound about the arms, held by six of de Brock's owl-hooters and to judge from the expression on Ox's ugly face things had certainly not gone according to plan.

This in itself Jess considered satisfactory for it meant that every available man was being used to keep Ox and his henchmen under surveillance. Further away, apparently engaged in an argument, was Fay. Before her, a smirk on his round, greasy visage, was tubby Mayor Anderson. On the porch, leaning against the rail and keeping things covered with a rifle, stood the guard who had watched over Ox and his boys in the living room. Nor did he seem particularly alert: he had the attitude of a man completely sure of himself.

Jess grinned. The situation was not so difficult as it had at first appeared. Turning, he raced back to his horse, took his lariat from the saddle-horn, and then returned to his vantage point. In the interval of his absence things had become more grim. Ox and his cohorts were being shoved in the direction of the blazing fire. They were struggling violently, trying in vain to protect themselves from its fierce heat as they came near to it.

Jess holstered his gun, poised himself, and then swung his rope carefully, his eyes fixed on the highest branch of the giant cedar tree in the yard. His ropework was good and the noose locked itself securely over the high branch. Whipping his gun back into his hand he twined the rope about his wrist and then leapt into the air.

Pendulum-wise, carried by the rope's swing, he hurtled across the yard. His legs tautly extended in front of him he crashed his heavy riding boots into the backs of the two men driving Ox and his boys towards the fire. Completely unable to save themselves they stumbled blindly forward, tripping and sprawling in the midst of the flames and searing wood, and dragging themselves up again with shrieks of pain.

Clean over the fire Jess travelled, released himself, and dropped. He twirled and fired twice with bewildering speed. The two remaining guards holding Ox and his boys crumpled, their guns flying out of their hands. The two other guards near the ranch-house fired blindly, once only. Then Jess' relentless gun got them one after the other.

A shot came from the rifle of the man on the porch. Jess saw the bullet hit the tree behind him. He grasped the rope again, hurtled himself back over the fire and crashed straight towards the porch. The guard saw the flying body coming and tried desperately to take aim. Instead iron-shod boots struck him a blinding blow in the face and sent him toppling from the porch into the dust below it. Jess dropped, grabbed the rifle and levelled it.

"Okay, take it easy!" he panted, as the two guards near the porch got up and the burned ones struggled into some kind of action.

"Get these blasted ropes of'n me!" Ox roared. Til durned soon wipe up this bunch, Jess! Hurry up, somebody, an' cut th' blasted things."

"Cut them free, Fay," Jess called to the girl, tossing over his penknife.

She nodded, caught the knife deftly, and in a few moments had released each man. Ox swung round, then without speaking any word or asking any questions he strode to where the guard had fallen. He was just getting to his feet, his face gashed and bleeding from where Jess' boot had struck him.

"What's th' idea, Ox?" Jess snapped, giving him a hard look. "There are more things t'do right now than bother with this critter."

"Not to me there ain't, Jess." Ox clenched his massive fists and glared. "He's a blabber-mouth! I happened t'say that yuh was with th' Calvert gal here an' this guy had ter repeat it to de Brock. I warned him what I'd do fur him fur openin' his trap too wide, an' now I aim t'do it!"

"Wait!" Fay cried, hurrying over. "Just a minute, Ox!" She caught his huge, blood-smeared arm as he retracted it to deliver a killing blow on the dazed puncher.

"Well?" Ox growled, obviously still disgruntled at the thought of a woman being mixed up in things.

"As we came here we saw de Brock heading away. D' you suppose he was going to my ranch?"

"He said he wus," Ox retorted. "To give you an' Jess a welcome home. Frum th' way things are I reckon he'll be mighty disappointed," he grinned.

"But my father's at home!" Fay exclaimed, horrified. "Heaven knows what de Brock may do to him!"

"That's right!" Jess gave a start. "We've got to get over to th' Calvert spread right away."

"An' leave these guys t'do as they like!" Ox gasped. "You gone nuts, Jess? Don't yuh know they've hanged the guy who ran this spread? An' his wife, too. In the stables back there. That's murder, an' it makes these skunks ripe fur a hangin', jus' like yuh said yuhself."

"We'll rope 'em up an' take 'em back to th' hideout with us. Later we'll hand 'em over to the authorities."

"Well, okay," Ox growled, unsatisfied, "but I'll be durned if I'm goin' t'be gypped outa payin' this guy a compliment. I've bin promisin' it to myself too long fur that!"

He considered the still semi-conscious guard. Then he spat on his right hand, doubled his fist, and landed the most frightful punch either Jess or the girl had ever seen. It sent the hapless man flying backwards. He hit the woodwork at the base of the porch and half fell through it, to lie motionless. Ox grinned and hitched his slipping pants.

"Okay, I'm satisfied," he said, shrugging. "Least, almost." With narrowed eyes he looked about him. "Where's the pot-bellied runt of a mayor gotten to? I've a bit uv a score t' settle with him, too."

"Yeah," Jess said, gazing around. "I'd like to say somethin' to that critter myself."

"There!" Fay cried, pointing. "Getting onto his horse."

Ox leapt forward, hurtled across the yard as fast as he could move, and flung himself at the mayor just as he was preparing to ride off. The grip on his collar dragged him out of the saddle and he crashed heavily to the earth. In a moment he was on his feet, hauled up by Ox's massive arm.

"Jess wants yuh," Ox explained sweetly. "When he's through with yuh then mebby I'll give your features a lift. Seems t'me they're a mite too flabby."

"I haven't done anythin'," the mayor panted, perspiring and wringing his hands. "Only as I was told. I didn't agree with it, though. It was de Brock's idea to drive you and your boys into the fire."

Ox spat. "Yeah. As I remember it it wus you who suggested shootin' us, wustn't it? Yuh big barrel uv eagle fat, I've a mind ter — "

"Take it easy, Ox," Jess ordered, curtly, coming up. "Take his rifle and keep these cut-throats covered. Get the rest of the boys to help you and tie these guys up good an' proper. I want a word with th' mayor here."

"A word? Nice an' pretty like? How's 'bout cigars an' a few drinks fur th' both uv yuh?"

"Shut up an' do as yore told!"

"Okay," Ox growled, and turned away. He aimed a sour look at Fay as she came running up. She caught Jess' arm.

"How about dad, Jess? We've got to be moving."

"We will, Fay, just as soon as these polecats are roped up. Now, Anderson, yore a pal of de Brock's, ain't you?"

"No!" the mayor retorted. "I do as he tells me, sure, even though I don't like it. I haveta, or take a slug where it'd hurt most. Not bein' crazy, I follows out orders. I guess any man who wants t'go on livin' would do just that."

Jess studied him. "Yeah, I can believe that. Yore not quite such scum as the sheriff was, or this bunch of cut-throats here. But as long as you take orders from de Brock yore not goin' to be mayor around here, see?"

"An' how d'you figger I can stop takin' orders from de Brock!"

"That's simple: you take 'em from me instead. If you don't I aim to blot you out. Plain enough, isn't it?"

"It isn't givin' a man a fair chance," Anderson complained. "If de Brock doesn't plug me, you will. That's what it comes to. I'm hog-tied either way."

"Yeah," Jess agreed calmly. "But with one difference. de Brock won't give you the ghost of a chance if he finds you've ratted on him. I'm prepared to let you keep alive and stay as mayor. But on one condition."

Anderson's flabby face lighted in sudden relief. "Okay. What's the condition?"

"That you hit the trail right now and fetch the State Governor from North Point City, an' take him to de Brock's spread as fast as y'can. You can make it all right, de Brock's used all the men he can spare to make the raid on this spread and guard his own place. So you shouldn't get plugged on th' way. If you come back with the Governor, okay. If you don't — " Jess gave a shrug. "Well, I reckon it'll be just too bad, that's all."

Anderson hesitated for a moment; then he nodded. "I'll try it, anyways. At least I stand a chance with things that way: I don't stand any with de Brock."

"There's one other thing," Jess added, catching the mayor's arm as he turned to go.

"Yeah?"

"As mayor of Yellow Gulch you have access to plenty of legal documents an' information which th' rest of us don't know about. How much can you provide t'prove that de Brock runs things his own way around here?"

"I-I guess I don't know," Anderson replied uneasily. "I ain't had much to do   with —"

"Get wise to yourself, Anderson. Your life depends on proving what kind of a no-account murderer de Brock is. Once you've started off to find the Governor you've

114

burned your bridges. So you might as well fix things as well as you can to make yourself safe on return."

The mayor considered this a few moments. "Well," he said, at last, "I might have quite a few documents which wouldn't improve things for de Brock if they became open knowledge. There are land deeds f'r example, showing the prices paid for some of the stuff de Brock's bought; copy wage-bills for his hired gunmen; lots of things like that … "

"They'll help," Jess said. "The rest of the stuff, the really vital stuff, will no doubt be in de Brock's own ranch, I suppose. Okay, give me your office key."

"Huh? Now just a minute, Burton — "

"Stop arguin' an' hand it over! Come on quick! You'll find it healthier."

Reluctantly the mayor did as ordered. Jess nodded and put the key in his shirt pocket.

"All right, Anderson, get on your way, and if you think of detourin' to warn de Brock, or escaping altogether to some place else, forget it! I'll find you if you hand me a double-cross, and when I do, heaven help you!"

"I'm not so crazy I don't know when a guy holds all the aces," Anderson retorted, turning away. He went across to his horse, scrambled up into the saddle, and spurred the beast away rapidly. Jess stood watching him go.

"How much more time are you going to waste, Jess?" Fay pleaded.

"Sorry, Fay. This had to be got going. I'm all set now, though. Got those boys nicely trussed up, Ox?"

"Sure have."

"Okay. Dump 'em on their horses an' let's get movin'."

7. The End of the Trail

Len Calvert was in the midst of sorting out the provisions he had brought back from town when the door of the ranch flew open and de Brock came striding through the narrow hall, his gun levelled. He gave a grim smile as he beheld Calvert standing looking at him in surprise.

"de Brock!" Calvert ejaculated, staring at him in surprise. "This is unnecessary violent intrusion."

"Save it, Calvert," the cattle baron interrupted, glancing about him. "Where's your daughter and Jess Burton?"

"I guess I ain't got a daughter any more," Calvert answered grimly.

"What the hell do you mean? You've had a daughter as long as I've known you. She isn't dead, is she?"

"Far as I'm concerned she might as well be." The rancher shook his head bitterly. "She's sold herself to the devil, and that's th' top an' bottom of it. The shame of it! That a daughter o' mine should go straight down to perdition an' — "

de Brock strode forward and seized Calvert by the lapel of his jacket, shaking him roughly.

"Stop spoutin' that psalmist drivel to me, Calvert, and come to the point. I want Burton, and I hear he's with your daughter. Now, where are they?"

Calvert set his mouth and hesitated before he answered.

"Last I saw of 'em they were in the grass, down the trail apiece. Jus' talkin', so they said, but I got my own notions about that. I warned my gal what she'd get if she ever came back here ag'in. She's dead, de Brock, far as I'm concerned. I never want t'set eyes on her again."

de Brock raised his eyebrows.

"Just because she's fallen for Jess Burton, and he for her?" Iron-hard, ruthless man though he was, de Brock at least had plenty of common-sense. "I always thought you were crazy, Calvert, and now I'm sure of it. Men and women have been falling in love since the world began, or didn't you get to hear of it in this neck of the woods? And a nice, blasted mess you've made of my plans, too, with your cockeyed notions on a girl's purity! I was expecting Burton to come back here with her, then I could have given them both a welcome."

"Why a welcome?" Calvert asked in perplexity. "What good has Burton ever done you?"

"None, and that's just the point. I've roped in all the rest of his boys, and now I want him — the biggest blackguard of them all. My welcome would have been at the business end of this." de Brock raised his gun, but the rancher looked at it unmoved.

"My gal knew I meant what I said," he stated, "and that bein' so she won't come back here, nor will Burton. So I reckon you've had a trip in vain, de Brock."

"Not necessarily." de Brock seated himself at the table and grinned ambiguously. "In fact, now I am here I might as well take care of some unfinished business. Come to think of it, though, it can wait 'til later. Right now my main interest is in Burton. Your girl being so thick with him she must know whereabout he's hiding out, eh?"

"Y' say you've captured Burton's men?" Calvert asked. "Well, what makes you think Burton'll ever go back to his hide-out with all his men gone? Wouldn't be sense, would it? The man's a saddle-tramp, sure, but he isn't plain crazy."

"It makes sense because as yet he doesn't know that I've captured his men. Since he won't be returning here with your daughter the only other place he can go is the hideout. So, where is it located?"

"My gal said somethin' about it bein' in the mountain foothills, but I don't know where exactly. I don't think she did either."

"That'll cover it nicely," de Brock said, his icy smile still there. Then he added, "For a self-professed religious man you haven't much idea of loyalty, Calvert, have you? Not even to your own flesh and blood? I'm no lily-white saint myself and never pretended to be, but I never give away my own folk."

Calvert's lean and colourless cheeks flushed. "Meanin' what exactly?"

"Meaning that you don't think twice about telling me where I can find the man your daughter loves and blot him out. Making sure you keep your own halo fixed straight, aren't you?"

"He took my gal away from me and he's against you," Calvert answered stubbornly "That means I don't care how soon you find him, or what y'do with him."

"Mmmm ... Apparently your daughter loves him quite a lot. How would you react, I wonder, if she remained so staunchly loyal to him that she died too? It could happen, you know, quite accidentally, of course."

"She sold her soul to him," Calvert banged the table. "So she must take what goes with it! I told her that straight!"

"You damned, lily-livered humbug!" de Brock said in contempt. "Burton's my enemy, sure, and I'm out to destroy him, but at least I've got a sense of values. I've always had a contempt for religion, and now I look at you, who've studied it all your life, I'm mighty glad of it. Just to satisfy your own vanity you tell me all I want to know and sell out your own daughter and the man she loves. To put it bluntly, Calvert, you stink!"

"What d'you expect me to do?" Calvert demanded. "Fight you when all the power's on your side?"

"Yes, certainly I do!" It was de Brock's turn to thump the table to emphasize his words. "Fight me the same as any real men would, the same as Burton's doing, blast him! He's clever, and he's got courage, and unless I'm mighty quick he'll do what he's set out to do and break my hold over this territory. If he does … "

de Brock mused over this for a moment and then shrugged.

"Well, if he does, okay. But at least he's worth fighting. Not like you." de Brock studied the rancher's cadaverous face. "That leaves only you on this ranch, Calvert, an' I've no time for a sniveller. You can pack your traps and quit by sundown. I'll have my boys see to it that you do. If you don't they'll have orders to blast hell out of you. Pray to your Maker, get on your knees, do what the blazes you like but be out by sundown, that's all!"

de Brock turned to the door, then as a further thought struck him he swung round. Only just in time he saw Calvert level a heavy .45 at him. de Brock fired instantly. The gun clattered out of Calvert's hand to the table. He swayed forward, clutching the table edge for support.

"Serves me right, mebby," he muttered. "I shouldn't ha' done that. Those who live by th' sword … perish by th' sword."

His hold gave way and he crashed to the wooden floor, de Brock stood looking, slowly holstering his gun.

"Misguided dimwit," he growled. "Guess I'll have to get th' boys over here to take the remainder of the cattle. What other stuff there is can be burned and a fresh start made. Nothing else for it."

He departed, descending the steps to his horse. Digging in the spurs he sent the animal swiftly along the trail which led to the looming mountain range nearby.

*

Perhaps half an hour later Jess, Fay, Ox, and their followers came riding into view, whilst behind them, their wrists roped to their saddles, came the hoodlums who had been so hopelessly beaten for the second time.

"Things look quiet enough," Fay said, contemplating the ranch as she slid from the saddle. "In fact, rather too quiet! I distrust it."

Jess jumped to the ground and joined her, leaving Ox in charge of the prisoners. The girl beside him, Jess mounted to the porch, frowned as he saw the door open, and then walked into the living room. There was nobody present. On the table was a big brown bag full of groceries.

"Dad!" Fay called, going back into the hall. "Dad, are you about anywheres?"

There was no response.

The girl looked into the bedrooms and then came back into the living room to find Jess staring thoughtfully at the wooden floor. In a moment she saw what had attracted his attention. There was a trail of crimson spots leading to the doorway. And, as he went further they led out across the hall and then lost themselves on the darker, sun-blistered wood of the porch.

"Do you think — " Fay stopped, mounting anxiety in her eyes as she looked at Jess.

"I dunno, Fay." He cuffed up his hat and gazed about the sun-drenched landscape. "Pretty plain that somebody got hurt, and very recently, too, since the blood's fresh. Whether it was your dad or old man Brock who got the works I can't say." He cupped his hands and shouted. "Hey there, Mr Calvert! You there? Mr Calvert!'

There was no answer from the silent wastes. Only the soft, hot wind and the stir of grass. Ox glanced over inquiringly from his horse.

"What gives, Jess?" he enquired. Jess told him, adding: "We"d better look around and see ii we c'n find Mr Calvert any place. Jim, Harry, you c'n help us. The rest of you stay where you are."

The search began immediately, but though they looked for a full hour, no sign of old man Calvert was found. Fay, sick with worry, at last came drifting back to her horse with Jess walking beside her in silence.

"There's one possibility," he said, after a spell of thought, "de Brock may have taken your father on his horse, since your dad's horse is in the stable, perhaps to hold him as a hostage or somethin'. Mebby he plans somethin' like your father's safe return for you handing me over, de Brock's up to any move on the board, remember. Anyways, there's nothing more we can do here. Our next job is to find out what happened to de Brock, an' also call in at the mayor's office and dig out what information we can which may be useful evidence for the Governor when, and if, he turns up."

"All right," Fay sighed. "Just as you say."

"At the moment," Jess added, when he had lifted her into the saddle, "we have one supreme advantage, Fay. de Brock doesn't know that his little ambush has come unstuck. That may give us just the final opportunity we need."

*

Whilst the search to find Calvert was proceeding, de Brock was riding cautiously up the narrow trail which led from the valley to the mountain foothills. He kept his gun constantly in his hand, his pale eyes darting about him quickly as he travelled.

For over two hours he wandered his horse in and out of the tortuous trails and arroyos and failed to find anything interesting. Then he stopped for a while in the shadow of a rock and lunched off the emergency ration in his saddlebag, also feeding his horse and watering him at a nearby stream. He had just come to the end of his meal when, in happening to glance upwards, he caught sight of a solitary figure on a rock far overhead.

The figure turned slowly, surveying the scenery, de Brock kept well hidden, watching. Then drawing carefully into the shadows he settled his revolver in a niche of the rocks and took careful aim. The report of the

123

gun echoed and re-echoed and the solitary figure fell flat on the spur and remained motionless.

"If Burton's somewheres up there he'll certainly come and see what happened to his look-out," de Brock murmured to himself, staring intently upwards. "If he doesn't I'll go an' get him in any case."

For over ten minutes he waited, but nothing happened; so he decided to take a chance. Leading his horse he went slowly up the trail, revolver in hand, prepared for any sudden attack from a hidden watcher above.

Entirely unmolested he reached the top of the acclivity and stood looking about him. The man he had shot down, Jed, who had been left on look-out by Ox, lay where he had fallen. A brief examination satisfied the cattle baron that the puncher was dead.

Returning to the trail he peered inside the cave, summing up the evidence it afforded. That it was a hide-out was beyond question: so there remained nothing but to conceal his horse and wait for Jess, perhaps with Fay Calvert, to put in an appearance.

At first de Brock squatted on the rock just inside the cave, eagerly expectant, his gun ready.

Then he relaxed somewhat as nothing happened. By the end of the afternoon he was yawning with boredom; and by late evening he could stand it no longer.

Impatiently he strode out on to the mountain trail and gazed about him. There was nothing but silence and the incredibly beautiful colours in the western sky. Slowly it was forced upon him that for some reason Jess was not returning to the rendezvous.

"I don't see how he could have known I'd be here," he mused. "Unless he did go back to the Calvert ranch after all and old man Calvert had enough life left in him to tell him what I'm aiming to do. Don't think he would though; not in the mood he was in. No purpose in sticking here. Have to get the boys together an' find Burton, wherever he is. The victory isn't complete without him corralled."

He turned to his horse, swung into the saddle, and rode quickly down the trail to the pasture-lands, striking out southwards when he gained the valley side, heading in the direction of his own Square-8. The sun had completely set when he arrived, and, with the swiftness common to the region, the evanescent twilight turned into starry night as he descended from his horse in the yard.

He paused for a moment, looking about him. There was a peculiar quietness about his spread which he could not understand, an intense, heavy silence. What noise there was came from the cattle in the corrals.

"Digby," he shouted, raising his voice. "Hey, Digby! You around?"

Digby, his new foreman, and one of those who had been raiding in the morning, failed to appear from the nearby bunkhouse. That building, too, was unusually dark and silent.

Puzzled, his gun in his hand as a precaution, de Brock took his horse with him to the stable, unsaddled it, and frowned still more as he saw that all the horses which had been used in the morning were in their stalls, nodding sleepily. The men had evidently returned all right, then.

Scenting danger, yet failing to see it, de Brock went over to the bunkhouse and peered inside. All was in darkness, something which had never happened before. He struck a match and ignited the nearest lamp. It cast a pale radiance over a deserted scene.

de Brock departed again, looked at the dark ranch-house, and then he settled his gun more firmly in his hand. He had never been a man who lacked courage, and it did not desert him now. Without any attempt at being quiet he strode up the steps, across the porch, wrenched open the screen-door and hammered on the inner frame. To his surprise the door opened immediately, the catch being broken.

"Elsie!" he called, peering into the dark hall and wondering if his wife were present. "Elsie, you there?"

There was no reply. Not a sound in the blackness.

De Brock muttered something to himself, felt for and lighted the oil lamp on the hall table; then carrying it at shoulder level he entered the living room and looked about him. He had just time to notice that his wife was seated near the table, staring at him fixedly. Then she gave a sudden hoarse shout.

"Look out, Wil — !"

De Brock swung, but not quickly enough. A rope whirled out of the dark and settled over his shoulders, pinning his arms. A hand reached out and took the lamp. Another hand whipped the gun from his fingers.

A shadowy figure leapt up and lighted the oil lamp hanging from the ceiling joist; then the lamp de Brock himself had been holding was carried to the table and set down. Jess turned the light full on the side of his face, throwing his high cheekbones and powerful jaw into a relentless profile.

"Why the hell could't you have shouted sooner?" de Brock demanded of his wife.

"Because she had a gun trained on her," Jess answered. "An' even if it was she took her life in her hands yellin' a warnin' to you like she did. She's more loyal to you than you deserve, de Brock!"

The cattle baron relaxed, his arms still pinned. A glance to the rear assured him that Ox was looming there, grim-faced, ready for any action that might be needed. In other parts of the room figures which had been in the shadows were now revealed, every one of them Jess' own men, and Fay Calvert.

"Pretty!" de Brock commented dryly. "Very pretty! So you all hid until I came in; then you sprang this on me. About what I might have expected from you, Burton!"

"Since you might ha' expected it it's a pity you weren't better prepared," Jess answered. "I haven't the least doubt but what, had you bin given the same chance, you'd have prepared a similar welcome for me an Miss Calvert. I happened to think the faster, that's all. You might like to know that your raid on the Crooked-Y was interrupted. Two of your men were shot dead; two others were badly burned. You'll find every one of your men in the room yonder, roped, and those that were burned have bin bandaged up. As for your beloved mayor he's gone to North Point City for the State Governor, and when he comes back my job's done far as yore concerned. You've come to th' end of th' trail, de Brock. I've got you licked!"

"Like hell you have! You don't suppose a few ropes an' a bunch of your damned gunmen can hold me, do you?"

"They help, but they're not everything," Jess agreed. "What really nails you is the evidence I've piled up. There was quite a lot of it in the mayor's office, to which he gave me th' key, and there was even more in your safe there."

De Brock twirled in sudden anger and stared towards the heavy safe standing on ornamental legs in a corner. Its door was swinging wide.

"Save your breath," Jess suggested cynically. "We opened the safe, or at least Ox did, and took out your personal papers. They lay everythin' bare, your whole rotten scheme for drivin' th' settlers outa this valley. Since yore not averse to takin' things yourself you can't blame us for doin' likewise. In fact, de Brock, you've hog-tied yourself completely. While you were so busy lookin' for me I came here with my boys, took care of those you'd left around on guard, and now yore where I want you. There's enough dope piled against you to hang you a dozen times over."

De Brock said nothing. Then he looked at Fay as she snapped a vicious question at him.

"What did you do to my father?"

"I shot him before he could shoot me. An' I reckon the world is well rid of a hypocrite like him."

"Yore trouble is that yore a bit too free in decidin' who's not wanted in this world," Jess snapped. Then glancing about him he added, "Pull that lariat off him, boys, and tie him up properly. After that dump him in the other room with the rest of the stiffs."

He stood watching intently as Ox and the boys went to work to remove the ropes from the cattle baron's arms. Mrs de Brock, however, edged her hand a little nearer to the lamp on the table. It was at the moment that the lariat was freed from her husband's shoulders that she acted. Whirling the lamp up she flung it at Jess as he stood not two yards away.

He gasped, dropping his gun as searing glass and burning oil exploded over him. Though he was not hurt, his upflung arm having protected him, he had completely lost the initiative, de Brock hurtled forward, snatched up the fallen gun and levelled it. He spent a moment or two trampling over the flames on the floor; then he looked about him through the smoke haze.

"Come over here," he instructed his wife; and when she had moved to his side he added, "Go and untie those boys of ours in the next room. Mebby this game isn't quite so played out as our cocksure friend seems to think!"

Smiling to herself, Mrs de Brock crossed the room and opened the nearby door. Jess watched her movements with grim eyes, his hands raised in common with the rest of the men and Fay. The cattle baron considered them, keeping well away to avoid any chance of a sudden spring. Then he looked up expectantly as his released men came trooping out one by one from the adjoining room.

"Take the guns from these men," de Brock ordered. "Use them yourselves since you're unarmed."

This was done, the men grinning at the complete turning of the tables.

"Now, Burton, I'll trouble you for that evidence you've collected concerning me," de Brock said, coming forward.

Jess only tightened his mouth in response.

"All right, if you wish to be obstinate," de Brock shrugged. He turned to one of his gunmen. "You," he ordered, "take a look around. These hoodlums have their horses concealed somewheres about the spread. Ten to one the papers I want are in one of the saddle-bags."

The man nodded and headed for the door. Just as he reached it Ox lunged suddenly and landed a smashing uppercut. It sent the gunman crashing back against the table, his head spinning, de Brock fired. There was a grim silence as Ox's giant figure dropped heavily to the floor and lay motionless.

"I never did like that overgrown ape," the cattle baron commented, blowing a wisp of smoke from his revolver muzzle. The half-stunned gunman picked himself up. de Brock watched him grimly. "You okay again?" he said. "All right, carry on. We'll wait."

He moved to the centre of the room and stood lounging against the table, his wife next to him. Then he said:

"Come to think of it, boys, you'd better get these tramps roped up. I've got plans for them, and we'll have to work fast in case that mayor returns with the Governor after all. When he does he and the Governor are in for a surprise."

His men turned back into the bedroom to get the ropes with which they themselves had been bound. In a moment or two they had returned. Jess was debating whether or not to risk the guns and make a fight for it when something happened. Wilton de Brock abruptly turned an almost complete somersault and landed on his back with teeth jarring-impact.

Simultaneously Ox leapt upwards, holding the carpet strip in his hands which he had jerked from under the cattle baron. Now he flung it over de Brock's head, smothering him with it.

"Grab your chance, Jess!" he yelled. "We've got 'em!" and regardless of guns or anything else he slammed out with his mighty fists.

Two of the gunmen went spinning into the bedroom, hurled into the dresser and toppled over on the floor with the dresser on top of them. The remaining men, slow-witted at the best of times, waved their guns uncertainly, afraid to shoot for fear they hit the struggling, swearing de Brock. Against the window his wife watched helplessly.

Jess swung, his fists ready, and lunged with all his power. In a matter of seconds he and the rest of the boys were slamming hammer-and-tongs, taking and receiving killing punishment as they reeled and swerved about the big room, the single oil lamp in the ceiling casting a yellow glimmer over the violence.

Ox, the most powerful member in the outfit, went down for the count as a chair was broken in pieces over his bullet head. Jess, turning to look at him, stopped a blow under the jaw which knocked him off his feet and dropped him half senseless on the floor. By the time he was able to see properly again he realized that the battle was lost. Panting but triumphant, de Brock's men were grouped around their boss as he stood by the door with twin guns levelled.

"You seem to like making things tough for yourself, Burton," he said bitterly. "This time I shan't give you the chance. I didn't think Ox had enough brains to play dead and pull the carpet from under me." He looked at the giant puncher as he got dizzily to his feet, holding his head. "Anyway, it's my trump this time. I don't see why I should waste time trussing you up before finishing you off. I'd planned to do that and dump the lot of you in the desert where you could never be found. As it is shooting you may be safer."

He paused as the gunman he had sent out to look for the papers came in, his arms full of documents neatly bound in tape.

"Good!" de Brock murmured. "Put them on the table. As I was saying, Burton, shooting's the only safe way, and that includes you, Miss Calvert. I don't say that I particularly like the idea of wiping out a good-looking girl like you, but you know too much, so I can't let you go free."

"If you lay a finger on her, de Brock, I'll come back from the grave an' get you!" Jess breathed, scrambling to his feet.

"Stop talking like an idiot, Burton!" de Brock snapped; and in the brief ensuing silence there was the faint sound of the gun-hammers coming up. The muzzles of his guns swung round directly at the girl and Jess.

But the shots were not fired. Instead there came the explosion of a gun from the hall, de Brock remained like a statue for perhaps three seconds, a faraway look in his pale eyes. Then his knees gave way and he dropped flat on his face.

Immediately two of his men rushed towards him, but they fell back as a tall figure came into view, a gaunt, dust-streaked figure of a man, blood dried on the front of his shirt.

"Dad!" Fay cried hoarsely. "Dad, it's you! Oh, thank God!"

She raced across the room and caught at his arms.

"Don't pull me, gal," he said briefly. "Liable to deflect my aim. Jess, you'd best get these critters roped up good an' pretty, hadn't you!"

"Yeah." Jess gave a surprised glance at the use of his first name. "Let's get busy, boys."

He turned to the task, Ox helping him. Then suddenly Calvert's gun swung round to Mrs de Brock as she sidled towards the door.

"Better hold it, ma'm," he said curtly. "We're not decided yet on what we're goin' to do with you."

"Dad, you're talking as though you really mean it!" Fay said tensely. "You're holding guns and fighting. Like I've always wanted you to."

"Yeah." He grinned a little. "I reckon Scriptures ain't much use to a man out here when a guy plugs you like this guy de Brock did. He got me in the shoulder, nothin' much, even though it looks bad. I decided I'd best get him in return. So I came, keeping outa sight when you searched for me so's I could spring a nice surprise when I wanted. I didn't use a horse, neither, 'case it was seen."

"From the sound of things," Jess said, "you've different views now in regards to Fay and me."

Calvert nodded. "I sure have, son. Besides, I've bin thinking. I'm going to need a strong man an' a lot of his pardners to build up my outfit now de Brock's bin taken care of. I guess you, and Ox, and the rest of 'em can help me plenty, an' all th' other ranchers who need it."

"In between my duties as sheriff, yes," Jess agreed, with a broad smile. "If I'm elected — "

"If!" Ox bellowed. "Huh! We'll pin back the ears uv every critter in town 'til you are! An' say," he added, "I just had a look at de Brock here, he's cashed in his chips, I reckon. Yuh got him clean, Calvert."

For a moment nobody spoke, then Jess looked up sharply.

"That sounds like two horsemen comin'. Must be the mayor an' Governor, I expect. An' the way things are it looks like we finished th' job ourselves."

"You mean you did," Calvert said quietly. "I'd never have tried it without somebody blazin' th' trail first." He looked at Fay earnestly. "I take back what I said, gal. This is one hundred per cent man yore gettin'."

"An' one hundred per cent gal," Jess responded, putting an arm about her shoulders.

Printed in Poland
by Amazon Fulfillment
Poland Sp. z o.o., Wrocław